A Festive Surprise

Margaret Amatt

LEANNAN
PRESS
INDEPENDENT PUBLISHER

LEANNAN PRESS

SCOTTISH ISLAND ESCAPES
A Quick Note

Welcome to the Isle of Mull – setting for the *Scottish Island Escapes* series

This series is loosely connected to The *Glenbriar Series* which is set after this series, but all the books can be enjoyed as stand-alones or in order – whichever you prefer!

There are some crossover characters throughout both series and hopefully you'll enjoy catching up with some familiar faces as well as meeting some new friends.

Happy reading!

For Lyn Williamson, without whom this series wouldn't exist

ARABIC WORDS USED IN THE BOOK

sadikati – my friend (referring to the car)

marhaba – hello

ya'ni – I mean/ well (stalling or filling phrase)

ah, mashallah, mashalla – Yay! I did it (not wanting to jinx future efforts)

ay / ay, na'am – yes

la, la, la – no, no, no

fe sehetak – cheers

jamilati – my beauty

wallāh – by god

bahebek, jamilati – I love you, my beautiful

ana bahebak – I love you (female to male)

ana bahebek – I love you (male to female)

yina'an – dammit!

baba – dad

mama – mum

ya lahui – oh no (when something is horrifying and amusing at the same time.)

id milad sa'id – Merry Christmas

inshallah – god willing (said in place of no to avoid an absolute negative)

With thanks to Jina S. Bazzar for the translations

Chapter One

Farid

Farid screwed up his eyes and gripped the steering wheel, turning it wildly. An early grave loomed towards those rocky cliffs. He pumped the footbrake, bringing the old pickup truck to a standstill. Back home, on the roads around Daraa with olive trees and sun-baked rocks lining the way, ice wasn't a problem. But here... different story.

He drew in a deep breath, tugged the gearstick into reverse and backed the truck away from the edge. The wild ocean pounded below. After what he'd been through this year, he was damned if he would let a force of nature get him.

Slowly, he rolled the truck along the bumpy track and over the crest of a hill. A large white house lay below in the untamed landscape. He pulled up outside the building, his hand still shaky. A sleek midnight-black lantern with a scrolled bracket hung above the door. The textured glass panes detailed with leaded diamonds reflected the low sun. He locked the handbrake. No need to mention what had just happened.

'Between you and me, *sadikati*.' He tapped the steering wheel.

He climbed out of the pickup and the wind whipped off the sea. A gust tore past, slamming the door. He leapt sideways just in time. A white-crested breaker roared up and split over the wall at the end of the long garden. Freezing air stung his cheeks and he rubbed his palms together. The crashing beat of the waves and the salty air carried memories. Holidays. Free time. Family. Days from another life. He loosened the straps on the giant tree belted onto the back of the pickup.

After unclipping the last buckle, he shielded his eyes from the sun, so bright yet so cold but it blessed the sea with a rich turquoise hue. Like in Latakia. The landmass rolling around the coast of this island wasn't dissimilar, but the buildings and trees were very different. Those blue waters could pass for the Mediterranean – colour wise anyway. Farid didn't fancy taking the temperature test. Imagine even putting a toe into that icy water. Brr. It chilled his blood, sending a shiver coursing through him and he pulled up the collar of his shirt.

Back to the tree. Farid tugged at the giant. Its rough bark chafed against his calloused hands. How to get this into the house? Would it fit? He ran his gaze over the doorway, sizing up the logistics. Monarch's Lodge was an apt name for this beautiful building. It certainly was fit for a king. But apparently it took its name from a mighty deer that once roamed the grounds. Maybe one day he'd meet such a creature. But right now, the tree. He squinted at it and rolled his shoulders.

'You must get in there.' He rubbed his close-trimmed beard. 'And without prickling me.' Taking its weight on his shoulder, he dragged it from the pickup and propped it up. No way was he getting this monster inside on his own. He strode up to the front door, dusting pine needles from the red and black checks on his shirt. Pulling up the collar, he held the soft fleece lining to his neck. Luxurious. Possibly brand new. What a long time since he'd had anything this good. He knocked, cocking his head at the mottled windowpane. Music drifted faintly from inside and people laughed. 'It's the Most Wonderful Time of the Year'. The words of the song filtered in and he tried to translate them. His English was reasonable and improving all the time, but the song was too fast to catch the subtleties.

The door opened and a young woman beamed at him with wide red lips. 'Hi, Farid.'

'Hi, Georgia.'

'I didn't hear the truck.' Georgia tucked a strand of blonde hair from her tousled bob behind her ear. She and her husband were his new employers. And good people. Thankfully. Georgia's smile was a permanent fixture and her husband, Archie, was generous. The shirt – and many more new clothes – had come from him. Farid had a home with four walls and a roof, thanks to their kindness.

'It's ok. I just arrived.'

'We had music on. We were dancing.' Her cheeks glowed and she fanned her face.

'Nice.' More than. Blissful in fact. To stop for a moment and dance with someone you love. So simple yet so special.

'Hello.' Archie appeared behind Georgia, smiling, and put his hand on her shoulder.

Farid massaged his palm over the left side of his chest, suppressing a growing ache spreading from his lungs to his heart. The empty cavities of his soul craved to be filled with a special person of his own. A real home with no doubts. One that nobody could take or send him away from. He pinched his lips together and looked at his feet. Finding that was like catching stardust. *Head down, fit in and survive.* Once he'd nailed that, he could work on the details.

'Is that our tree?' Archie said.

'Yes. I can't lift it alone.'

'No worries.' Archie stepped outside, clapping his hands together. 'It's bracing out here.'

Georgia followed them and inspected the tree. 'Oh, I love it. It'll be perfect in the hall. Can I show you where I want it? Then I have to shoot. I'm setting up Santa's grotto at The Boat Shack.'

Farid blinked. 'The what?'

'Come and see when it's done,' Georgia said. 'It's magic.'

'She'll have you dressed as Santa yet,' Archie said.

Farid smiled. 'Years ago, before the bombs, I go to Damascus with many friends. I see a big Christmas tree.' He raised his hand skyward. How tall and proud it stood in the Christian quarter.

'What a sight. And the lights.' He clung to the pictures burned into his memory. Anything of his homeland before the dark days.

'It sounds beautiful,' Georgia said.

'Very. But I still don't much get this Christmas.'

'I'll explain sometime,' Georgia said. 'But it could take a while.'

'Christmas has grown arms and legs since the nativity,' Archie said.

Christmas with arms and legs? What? Sometimes this language had the oddest sayings. Farid shouldered the tree and, together with Archie, they lugged it into the house. With some toing and froing, they manoeuvred it into the stand.

'There.' Farid stepped back.

'Perfect.' Georgia grinned and brought her hands together under her chin.

Perfect, huh? Maybe in her eyes. Farid furrowed his brow. One day, someone might explain the point of bringing a cut tree into the house. And how did it fit with baby Jesus and a man in a red suit? If assimilating into Scottish culture meant understanding it, he had an enormous mountain to climb. Cuddly toys of the Loch Ness Monster were one thing, glittery reindeer, quite another. And don't get him started on the food – deep-fried chocolate bars. Just why?

'Right, I better be off,' Georgia said. 'And I mustn't forget.' She nipped into the open-plan kitchen area and grabbed a large shopping bag. 'Carys is going to call in for this elf outfit. She wants to see if it fits. I hope it does; I need an extra elf for Santa's grotto.'

Archie frowned. 'I won't be here either. I have my meeting this afternoon.'

'Oh, drat.' Georgia face-palmed. 'I forgot. I won't be too long. Holly's arriving later too…' She checked her watch.

'I can wait,' Farid said. 'I see some logs at the front. I can cut them.'

'That would be amazing, thank you.' Georgia patted his arm. 'You're a superstar.'

'I'll pop that on your wages,' Archie said.

'Thank you. But no need.'

'You deserve it.' Archie clapped his back. 'Saves me a job.'

Farid shut the pickup's tailgate and waved off Georgia and Archie. Behind the house, the land rose steeply, providing a sheltered backdrop. Farid opened the woodshed and scanned around for the equipment. His gaze fell on a stack of plastic boxes at the door. Silver and gold sparkles bulged against the translucent sides. He lifted a lid to reveal strings upon strings of glittery tinsel, fake icicles, and lights. On top was a neatly folded red hat with white fur around the base. Santa's hat. Santa! He smirked. That bizarre chubby man with his red suit who featured in shop window displays. Farid lifted out the hat and put it on. Now he must look the part. His beard was black and neat, unlike the bushy white one belonging to the strange man. He patted his gut – not even one ounce of extra fat. What would his parents make of this? Stepping outside, he snapped a selfie. His sisters would appreciate it.

Grabbing the axe and a saw, he returned to the front of the house and pulled out the first log. Lifting the axe, he caressed the handle, then raised it above his head. It came down with a thump. Two bits of wood sprang apart.

'*Ah, mashallah, mashalla.*' He laid the next section out.

Chopping logs was the main deal in his new forestry job, though usually with more sophisticated equipment. He brought the axe down hard again and the wood split clean. With a crisp nod, he tossed the log into the basket and grabbed another.

A chainsaw was easier but manual work released tension in his body and mind. Pent-up energy thrummed inside him. Acceptance fought anger. The desire to fit in battled with a desperation not to forget or lose who he was. He cracked another piece of wood, straightened up and wiped his brow. The wind caught his face and the Santa hat blew off.

He snatched it off the ground and shoved it back on. Down came the axe with another satisfying thud. Whatever was happening in this crazy world, he at least could be grateful for some simple pleasures.

Chapter Two

Holly

The radio crackled and fizzed as Holly sped along the side of Loch Awe, heading west. Tall mountains capped with snow on either side reflected on the glassy surface. She punched the volume down but didn't switch it off. A call could come through on the handsfree at any time.

The likelihood of reception was verging on zero but work didn't stop – no, not even in the car. Her software design client waiting list was out of the building and down the street. Ideas and solutions whirred through her mind. Maybe her next project should be to create AI to drive the car for her while she carried on working.

She rounded a corner and slammed on the brakes. 'Holy shit!' An ancient low loader had stopped in front. Its hazard lights flashed orange. Lying in the road between it and Holly's car was a fully decorated Christmas tree. 'Seriously?' She gritted her teeth. Was there no escape from the bloody abomination that was Christmas? Why so early? November was too soon. She squeezed the bridge of her nose and groaned. The next month couldn't come and go fast enough. Roll on January.

The truck door opened. Holly's jaw almost hit the immaculately clean floor of her BMW X5. A rotund man in a red suit jumped out and jogged up the road, rosy cheeks beaming and belly waggling.

'No way,' Holly said. 'Just no way.'

With a jolly wave, he picked up the tree, hauled it onto the truck and strapped it down. Holly's mouth hung open as he trotted back to the cab and pulled off. Had that actually happened? She edged into first gear. Yup. There was the badly attached tree ambling around the twisty loch-side road in front of her. And Santa too. She tapped the wheel. If he moved this slowly come Christmas Eve, there would be a lot of disappointed kids in the world. She could relate.

'Can we get a move on?' she muttered. The Isle of Mull called – peace, tranquillity and remoteness. She'd had a fleeting visit earlier in the year for her friend's wedding. Now, it was exactly the place for an island escape. Georgia and her new husband had a big estate with cottages for rent and Georgia was happy to let Holly stay in one as long as she wanted. Friends like that were the best. The ones you didn't see often but picked up where you left off when you finally met again. Holly had a lot of friends like that... In fact, all her friends were like that. Some she hadn't met up with for a crazy long time.

The phone rang. Work. She hit the answer button on the dash. 'Hello... Yes, Holly Devaney speaking...' That autopilot needed to get bumped up her priority list, then she could take notes rather than trying to remember everything. She committed as much of the client's request to memory as possible. New software development projects were her favourites. They sparkled, pulling her attention away from current jobs and she couldn't help taking on far too much. When she ended the call, the radio flipped back on and the opening notes of 'Driving Home for Christmas' tinkled out.

'Oh, just go away.' She slammed the volume back down. She wasn't driving home for Christmas for two reasons. One, she hated Christmas. Two, she didn't have a home.

Once she'd boarded the ferry, she found a seat and opened her laptop, typing in details from the call and setting up a new folder of ideas for the client's software brief. Already inundated with projects, she could easily afford to lay off but work was life and she could handle it. People milled around but she didn't give them a second glance: her latest project was all she had eyes for. She'd barely started considering the features the clients would need in their app when the call came to get back in the cars. That was an hour? There weren't enough minutes in the day. She slammed her laptop shut, stowed it in her case and returned to the car.

The clouds above parted as she drove off the ship, leaving a pale, wintery blue sky. She followed the road north. It was imprinted in her brain from her last visit. That visit had been an eye-opener. She spent most of her life in cities and never settled anywhere, living mostly out of a suitcase as she had done since she was a child. What was the point of getting stuck in one place? Big open places like this, surrounded by the sea, were novel and fuelled a raw romanticism. Wow. That was new. Where had that notion come from? Practicality and rationality ruled her world. Mostly.

She passed through a village called Salen, then took a road west that cut across the island through rugged hills and woodland, finally descending into the picturesque village of Dervaig. The sea twinkled beyond.

Not too far around the coast, Holly arrived at the pillared gates of Ardnish Estate.

It was eight years since Holly and Georgia's uni days. They kept in touch through social media but at the wedding earlier in the year, it had felt like no time at all had gone by. Georgia was still her lovely, wacky self. But, eek, how her situation had changed. Who'd have thought she'd be the one to bag the lord of the manor and live in a place like this? At uni, she and Holly had been the life and soul of every party. Georgia hadn't let the world spoil her. Holly had grown up, got serious in business and made a career.

No regrets. The dull ache in her chest was just from sitting too long.

The main house was stunning. Maybe a tad austere and foreboding, like something from an Agatha Christie adaptation. Georgia and Archie rented it out as an island castle for luxury getaways. No doubt it appealed to lots of wealthy holidaymakers. The house they'd taken for themselves was equally gorgeous, perhaps more so because of its quaint location, tucked away on a rugged shelf at the bottom of a hill. Holly drove towards it, mesmerised by the sea as it crashed in from miles off, spritzing and foaming along the garden wall. Monarch's Lodge was a house from a fairy tale. Her heart curdled at the flicker of a memory. Once she'd dreamed of living in a place like that with a husband and two point four children, after the big white wedding and the exotic honeymoon. She knew better these days. Travelleritus had kicked in. Those dreams belonged to a different life. She had to find Georgia, get her to lead the way to the cottage, crack open the wine and chill. Simple.

Her foot pressed the brake pedal as she approached. A man in a red checked shirt and Santa hat was chopping wood at the front of the house. Seriously? WTAF? Was this Georgia's idea of a joke? Was that Archie? Had she sent him out to put on a display? Holly pulled up outside the door. It sat ajar and, Jesus Christ! Inside was a giant Christmas tree. She clung to the wheel, her knuckles whitening. Some crazy parties had gone down at uni. A vision of Georgia shimmying in a paper hat with tinsel around her neck flipped to the top of the memory pile… the finer details were lost to alcohol. Had Georgia always been Christmas crazy or was this a new thing?

Holly held her breath. Ok. Grin and bear it. Once she was in her cottage, she could shut the door and pretend none of it was happening. The beaches and hills were safe. No one could decorate them. Shaking her head, she turned her attention to the wood chopper. Her pulse stopped and a mini firework display kicked off in her chest. That wasn't Archie. Archie was a good-looking guy, edging to the better side of refined, but this man… Holy crap, this man was a drool-inducing Adonis. Dark curls swept around his forehead and a neatly trimmed beard accentuated his chiselled jaw. His shirt gaped open, displaying a wedge of gloriously golden-brown skin, gleaming with beads of sweat.

Holly rubbed the underside of her chin. *Close mouth now.* He was heading her way. Uh-oh. He tickled every fancy she'd ever had. No one had ever struck her like this with just one look. No way. If the house was empty, she'd drag him upstairs this minute. Jesus, shit! What was she thinking? Behave. Bloody behave. She pushed open the door and jumped out.

The man detoured towards the house, leaned inside and pulled out a large carrier bag stuffed with brightly coloured fabric. Clothes of some kind?

'*Marhaba*… Hello. I have here your elf costume. You can put it on and when it fits… er… *ya'ni*…' His eyes skimmed over her and he ran his hand through those lush curls. Holly would happily help. 'You wear it to Santa's grotto, yes?'

'Pardon?' Forcing her attention out of her imagination, Holly frowned. 'Why do I need an elf costume? Is this a joke?' Honestly? Did people want to shove Christmas down her throat and up her backside at the same time?

'No... I don't know. Georgia said I give you this and you can wear it.' He held out the bag.

'I'm not wearing that.' Her gaze locked with his. *Oh my god.* She might collapse. His eyes. How were they so blue? Not just blue but piercing and gorgeous. Elf costume be damned. If he wanted her to wear it, she would. Jeez, she'd do anything for those eyes. She was melting into a pool of liquid caramel and he could mould her into anything he wanted. Lick her up, eat her, literally anything.

He swallowed, rubbing his Adam's apple, and she blinked, reprimanding her wayward mind and putting herself on a short leash. This had to stop. She was thirty-two, successful and altogether sensible. This guy looked younger and she'd always disliked younger men. Just because. At least older guys had a chance of being more mature. The man lowered the bag and continued to stare.

'Why does Georgia think I want an elf suit?' She was the last person on the planet who would put on an elf suit. You wouldn't get her within ten metres of the ridiculous thing or anything else

Christmas related either. Not one single snowflake's chance in hell of that.

CHAPTER THREE

Farid

Farid gripped the bag straps, clutching them so tightly his short nails dug into his palms. The woman stared at him. And what a woman: tall, elegant, striking, and smartly dressed in a crop tweed jacket, skinny jeans and boots. Something in her greyish-green eyes warned him not to mess with her but the depth of her irises told another story. A sad one. He saw a similar story when he looked in the mirror. Her face held him like a magical force, commanding him. He was drawn forward.

'You're not the elf?' he said.

'Do I look like an elf?'

He shook his head. 'Too tall.'

'Exactly.'

He rubbed his free hand across the bare patch of his chest. The woman's gaze followed his movement. Heat throbbed within. The sweat he'd built up chopping wood spread. The woman trailed her fingertips along the smooth skin of her collarbone, just visible beneath her top. Did she like what she saw? He did.

He held eye contact, flicking up the corner of his lips. Stay cool. There were no expectations here. *Take things easy.*

Stepping forward, he pushed out his hand, forgetting the half-chopped log at his feet. He stumbled over it, almost losing his balance. The bag flew open and the contents spilled onto the ground. Bang went cool. An engine rumbled and Georgia's car trundled down the path. The woman pressed her fingers to her lips, stifling a laugh. Farid straightened his shirt. *Shit.*

'Are you ok?' She blinked between him and Georgia's car.

'*Ay.* Yes.' Farid snatched a pair of stripy leggings and shoved them back into the bag. The woman's stare burned into his back. He stooped to grab the red top; bells jingled and a sprig of plastic plant caught between two paving slabs. He tugged it up and pulled a face at it.

Georgia's car door banged.

'Hello, hello,' she said. 'Oh, by gosh by golly, it's mistletoe and Holly!' She threw out her arms and embraced the woman.

'Seriously?' The woman returned her hug stiffly. Over Georgia's shoulder, she arched an eyebrow at Farid, gave Georgia a quick pat on the back and pulled away.

'Loving the festive spirit,' Georgia said.

The woman's expression dulled. 'I don't do festive spirit.'

Farid scrambled to pick up the remaining items from the bag. When he straightened up, he zeroed onto the woman again. Her expression was detached. Farid edged closer, tilting his head and frowning. How could he make her smile? Ha! What was he thinking? She was nothing to do with him. But a murmur in his chest made him certain their paths would cross again.

Georgia grinned. 'I love Christmas.'

The woman drew back. 'I'm here to escape Christmas. I can't stand all the fuss. Didn't I say?' She peered at Georgia. Her chin jutted forward and her shoulders seemed tense. She rubbed her palm up the arm of her tweed jacket.

An urge to fill her world with magic burst through Farid's veins. Where were these thoughts coming from?

'I don't remember you saying you didn't love Christmas. Oops. I hope I haven't scared you off with my giant Christmas tree,' Georgia said.

The woman raised an eyebrow. 'You might have.'

'Please,' Farid said. 'Your pardon. I think I am the one scaring you. I thought you were the elf.'

Georgia raised her hand to her lips. 'Holly definitely isn't an elf.'

'I see now. Please, I ask you, don't go. My mistake. I apologise.'

Holly scanned him over, her cool eyes taking their time. No, she wasn't an elf; she was an ice queen. Her dark pupils froze his blood as they travelled over every inch of him. His body blazed with ice burns.

'All right,' she said. 'But keep me out of the Christmas prep.'

Georgia beamed and saluted her with a wink.

'I mean it. And I'd rather elf-suit-brandishing lumberjacks didn't accost me everywhere I go if it's all the same to you.'

What? The words were there but he couldn't translate them fast enough. 'You've lost me. I don't get the ways of this country yet.'

'Hardly surprising,' Holly said. 'People make up traditions left, right and centre, especially at this time of year.'

'Ah, we'll have you kilted up like a true Scot come Hogmanay,' Georgia said.

'A what?' Farid clenched his fist around the handles of the bag. What did she mean? Her smile said she was joking. Fine. But cold air echoed in the hollows of his chest. He'd left a rich culture and the warmth of a family behind. Lifting his right shoulder slightly, he looked back at Holly, doing a double take. Her gaze was glued to him. Her teeth grazed her lower lip, suckering him in the gut.

'It sounds ridiculous to me too,' she said. 'Where are you from?'

'Daraa.'

She gave a brief nod. 'That must be tough.'

'It is.'

'What's your name?'

'Farid Al-Karim.'

'Pleased to meet you.' She thrust out her hand. 'I'm Holly.'

Farid blinked before he took it. His grandfather would have frowned and tutted at shaking a woman's hand, but Farid's brief hesitation came from the formidable glint in Holly's eyes. Her grip was firm and she held on. An electric current surged up his arm. He clutched her cold palm, his jaw going rigid, but he couldn't break from her stare. Was she X-raying him or channelling his brainwaves?

'You'll be pleased to hear you're neighbours,' Georgia said. 'Farid's cottage is the other half of yours.'

'Is it?' Holly released his hand. His palm slipped from hers. Georgia nodded.

Nerves prickled up Farid's back. She was his new neighbour? The peace and quiet of his cottage had been absolute until now. Questions leapt into his head. Did she have a noisy job? Would she expect to call in for chats? How long was she there for?

'*Ya'ni,*' Farid said. 'I will see you about then. And I am sorry about the elf. I was mixed up.'

'I'll let you off.' Holly scanned his face again, dropping her gaze from his eyes to his lips, then back.

Was she being facetious? Rude? Flirtatious? All of them? A rude neighbour would be awful. A flirty one could be fun. But not sensible. His parents wouldn't want him carrying on relationships while he was here. Of course, he must live his own life as best he could, but old ways died hard. Adjusting was tricky enough without more complications.

He glanced at her. A half-smile played on her glossy pink lips. His gut swooped. He'd vowed to keep his head down, be safe and be sensible. Keeping himself to himself and getting by were his only goals... Or had been when he arrived. Was it still possible?

Chapter Four

Holly yanked her car into reverse and whipped around in the flat area in front of Monarch's Lodge. The wheels spun. 'Oh, it's icy.'

'Yeah, take care,' Georgia said. 'We don't get gritters down here.'

'Will I be able to see the sea from the cottage?' Holly powered into first gear.

'Sure.' Georgia strapped herself into the passenger seat. 'It's an old workers' cottage, so it doesn't have huge windows, but we're hoping to get planning permission for a conservatory. It'll make such a difference.'

Farid raised his hand as they drove past. Both Holly and Georgia returned it. 'Who is he?' Holly asked.

'Farid.'

'I heard that much. But what's he doing here?'

'He's a refugee.'

'Really?'

'Yeah. It took him four months to get to the UK, then he lived in hostels and on the streets.'

'Maybe I'm completely ignorant but I didn't expect to find refugees here. Weren't they relocated in the cities?'

'They've been rehoused all over Scotland. Farid's family knew Archie from when he worked for the oil industry.'

'I see. So, isn't that something different? An economic migrant?' *Listen to me!* Growing up with her dad, this kind of questioning was drilled into her. Did it even matter?

'No. He was persecuted and escaped. He came here as an asylum seeker and it was pure luck he knew someone in this country. We're both happy to help him out. It's the least we can do.'

'Totally.' Holly ran her fingers through her long brown hair, shaking it out as she drove one-handed up the track. Farid's plight sounded horrific but that thought got muddled with many more. How bloody distracting would it be with someone that gorgeous as a neighbour? 'What age is he?'

'Late twenties,' Georgia said. 'I'm not sure exactly. Why?'

'Because he's hot as sin and I need a good reason to keep my hands off him.'

Georgia laughed. 'Wow. You've done my job for me.'

'What job?'

'I love setting people up together.'

'Yeah. I'm not talking about marrying him. But having him just through a wall will be a struggle. He's the best-looking man

I've seen for a long time, so please tell me he's married and has a wife waiting for him back home.'

'No. He's single.'

'Oh Jesus. Wrong answer. Couldn't you at least have pretended?'

'Turn right up here.' Georgia chuckled into her hand. 'You only met him two minutes ago.'

Holly steered the car along another track close to the cliff edge with a low barrier.

'Long enough to get an eyeful.'

'You might not even like him. Maybe he's gay.'

'That's better,' Holly said. 'You're swinging it. Has he got some hidden nasties in his life? I mean, what did he do that he had to escape Syria?'

'Spoke up in the wrong place at the wrong time, I think. He's a charming, kind, helpful and all-round nice guy.'

'Not helping.' Holly tapped the wheel.

'Well, he did think you were an elf. So, if you're determined not to like him, keep remembering that.'

'I'm not determined not to like him. He's a stud muffin by the looks of things. I just don't want to get involved.'

'It wouldn't be a crime if you were to get together.'

'Nope. No entanglements, not with a neighbour. Far too awkward.'

'Really? You were always the one who wanted to settle down when we were at uni. You told me if you weren't married by twenty-six all sorts of dire things would happen.'

'Yeah. That was when I was young and stupid.'

'We all thought Gavin was the man.'

'Oh, please. Don't remind me of him.'

Georgia pressed her lips together with a smirk.

On a flat patch exposed to the elements was a long, low bungalow. A picket fence ran the length of the spartan front gardens separating two identical front doors. Was that all that would be between her and the Syrian hotcake?

'It gets windy up here,' Georgia said. 'But the cottages are fully done up, so they're cosy inside.'

Holly sucked the inside of her lip, silencing the thoughts assailing her brain. This was it? A tiny bungalow on the edge of a cliff. One gust might blow it into the ocean.

'I'm sorry,' Georgia said.

'No, it's fine.' Holly's thoughts must have shown on her face. And what did it matter anyway? She'd lived in so many places. This was just one more and out here might be the safest place in the world to avoid Christmas. There was nothing remotely festive about the place.

'But you haven't seen inside yet.'

'Oh? Is something wrong inside? Does the roof leak?'

'Er, no.' Georgia pulled a face. 'I kind of decorated it... I didn't realise you hated Christmas.'

'Right.' It was only November. What could she have done already? If it was fur blankets and candles, she could just about cope. 'I'm sure it'll be fine.'

Georgia opened the low gate and led Holly up the path. 'This is your key, but honestly, out here, no one locks their doors.' She flung open the door and Holly entered the tiny hallway. So far, so good. She pushed open the door to the living space and her eyes bugged out. Her breath caught and she balled her fists, barely containing a scream. There was a tree. An actual bloody Christmas tree. Wonderfully tasteful and in keeping with the décor but the whole place reeked of a tourist cabin in Lapland. If Mr and Mrs Claus were sitting by the fire, it would have looked perfectly acceptable.

Holly opened her mouth. Words failed. She frowned. What was she hearing? A low, jaunty tune. 'Deck the Halls' tinkled from a speaker system somewhere. Too much. 'Where's that coming from?' Her gaze darted around.

'Over here.' Georgia stepped up to a built-in shelf on one side of the fireplace and flipped a switch on the dock, lowering the volume. Foliage adorned the length of the mantelpiece, interspersed with candles and two decorative stockings hung at either end. Red tartan and deer scatter cushions were strewn over the cream sofa. A long, wrought metal candle holder of a reindeer pulling a sleigh sat atop the coffee table; each pair of deer and the sleigh had a votive set in it.

Holly's stomach tensed. She couldn't stay here. Not only was it stuck out on a limb, but this. *Ugh.* Mrs Sinclair would love this house. So would Gavin, her son. They were the perfect Christmas family after all. And Holly was the wrecker.

'I can take it all away,' Georgia said. 'Honestly, I don't mind. I was just having a bit of fun.'

Holly held her hand to her forehead and breathed deeply. Images of Christmas horrors streamed through her mind like unwanted ads on YouTube you couldn't stop until you'd watched. Mrs Sinclair's simpering sneer. Mr Sinclair saying grace. Gavin smiling across the table laden with sprouts and a turkey the size of a dolphin in centre place. The Christmas cake. The ring, sparkling and glinting with a cruel gleam. Gavin's horrified face. Mr and Mrs Sinclair's gaping mouths. A blade in the heart. Christmas carnage. 'Leave it. I might not be staying long anyway. There's a change of plan.'

'Oh. Really?' Georgia still smiled, but one side of her lip sagged. 'Because of Farid?'

'No, though it might be the only way to stop me jumping him. Just work.' Holly was well-practised in this dodge. 'I had a call earlier. I might have to shake things up. We'll see. Thanks for the effort you've put into this place.' Yes, no denying that. Just the sentiment.

'I'm so sorry if it offends you. I should have asked first.'

'No, it's fine. Don't think any more about it. It's gorgeous. Do you want a lift back to Monarch's Lodge?'

'No, I'll walk. It's not far. Are you ok here by yourself?'

'Perfectly. I can't wait to settle in.' The words flowed and she pulled out a smile but all she wanted to do was get out and run.

Georgia hovered on the doorstep. 'Don't be a stranger. We're happy to have you any time. If you're lonely, pop around. Or pop next door.' She winked.

'Yeah, thanks. I'm trying to avoid that, remember?' Holly waved to the giggling Georgia and watched until she was a dot on the path. *Now, slowly turn around and face the house.*

She collected her case first. Not a particularly large one. She had a neat set of outfits she chopped and changed. When they needed replacing, she replaced the whole set so everything mixed and matched. She fetched her laptop bag next, two garment carriers and a bag of food that wouldn't last more than two days. Even that small amount of luggage took up too much space in the tiny hall. She shuffled along, pushed open a door she assumed was the bedroom, and froze. 'No bloody way.'

A winter wonderland shone before her. Some princess some-where would love this. Someone in her own family even – her mother, her sister, her niece. 'But not me!' She shook her head. What a nightmare. How could she sleep in this? One night. She could do that. One night, then she was out of here. Where would she go this time? Who knew, but she couldn't bear it.

No point in unpacking. Even the food could stay in the bag.

Work. Do some work. It was the only thing that could make her feel better. Hauling out her laptop, she set it up in the abomination of a living room. Her arms relaxed as she opened the familiar programs and set her fingers typing. Better. Her breathing calmed as she focused on the lines on the screen. Time passed in a blur of codes, checkboxes and elements. The glitter fest surrounding her was just white noise in the background.

Bang! Bang! Bang! Holly jolted, almost dropping the laptop. 'What the hell?'

People came knocking? Out here? She placed the laptop on the coffee table and hurried to the door. It was solid wood with only the smallest diamond-shaped window, all mottled glass. So, who was it? She pulled it open and it dragged over the cream carpet. Her eyes connected with a pair of deep blue irises, and a pyrotechnic explosion ripped through her. What was he doing here? Had Georgia sent him to stir things up? This guy had crushing appeal. Maybe he felt the same. Was that why he was here? Her new neighbour popping around for the old cup of sugar. The Stone Age part of her brain had already cooked up a plan to grab his hand and drag him straight to the bedroom. Restraint. Stay calm. She tugged her lips into a fixed smile. 'Hi.'

'Hi,' he said.

'What can I do for you?' She adjusted the neckline of her sweater.

'Nothing.' He pulled a little shrug. His accent was cute. A deep voice tinged with uncertainty. 'I feel bad.'

Holly raised her eyebrows. 'Well, we can't have that. What's making you feel bad?' Her mind whirled on a carousel of ideas on how best to cheer him up – most of them wholly inappropriate, some of them completely X-rated. But would any of them work? A hint of desperation lingered in his expression. Here stood a soul almost as lonely as hers, crying out for love. She could sense it.

'The elf thing.'

She laughed. The sound surprised her. She was laughing about something Christmassy! 'No worries. Just forget it.'

His lips curled up. Oh crap. Her knees might give way soon. His mouth. His smile. His eyes. His hair. Oh, Jesus, Mary and the bloody donkey too. Everything about him was far too damned sexy and alluring to be allowed. Since when did men bother her like this? Even Gavin hadn't had this effect.

'I like to give you this. A gift for you. For making yourself at home.' He held out a box.

She took it and lifted the top. 'Er, what?' He had to be kidding her. Mince pies. Bloody mince pies. Perfectly formed down to the neatly cut holly shapes on top. Was this his idea of a joke?

'You don't like them?'

'What?' *Shit.* 'Oh, er, I'm sure they're great. But, I'm sorry. This probably sounds rude, but I don't like Christmas. All the hype irritates me. I didn't mean to be ungrateful. I just, arghh.' She thrust her hand into her hair. 'You know what? This was kind. Thank you. But it's wasted on me because I'm not staying. I'm leaving tomorrow. In fact, please tell Georgia for me. I don't want to have a long, drawn-out conversation about it. I just want to leave. I can't stay here.'

Mind made up. Now, shut the door. Her fingers gripped the frame, knuckles white, ready to push it closed and end this silly interlude in her life.

CHAPTER FIVE

Farid

If looks could kill, Farid would be lying at the bottom of the ocean. Holly's steely eyes had him in a grip lock. She was as prickly as the plant she took her name from. He squared his shoulders. Pull back? Let her go? Raw desire scorched him like a flaming ember.

The door swung forward. Farid put out his hand to stop it from closing. 'I don't understand. You want to leave because you don't like my pies?' He pulled up an eyebrow.

She glared for a second, then the iron look softened. 'It's nothing to do with the pies. I just don't like Christmas.' She glanced at the box. 'I haven't had mince pies for years.'

'These pies are not what you think. They aren't the odd things you have here. I make these from an old Syrian recipe but I like the idea of the holly on top. So, I cut it. Then I hear your name is Holly and I think of you. So, I come back and get them.'

'Ok.' Slowly she prised open the box lid again and peered inside, a slight frown creasing her smooth brow. 'What's in them then?'

'It's beef with spice, some pomegranate juice and...' He pinched his thumb and forefinger together. 'A little magic.'

Her lips quirked. The movement messed with his brain, scrambling his thoughts and rerouting messages to places not used to receiving them. Or dealing with them. *Keep cool.*

'All right, I'll let you off. They sound interesting. Thank you for thinking of me.'

He'd thought of nothing else for the last hour. Those sad eyes, her powerful stare.

His experience with women was negligible. Back home, hooking up and dating weren't easy, not in his family, where they stuck to traditional values. After he'd fled, relationships went too. Getting from place to place and surviving was enough. And now? Here, he was alone, isolated. Did he have to be? Looking was surely ok? And kindness cost nothing. How often he'd begged for crumbs of friendly conversation over the last year. Being looked down on as the scum of the earth as people rushed past, too busy to even notice yet another homeless refugee at their feet.

'Would you like to come in?' she asked. 'We could eat these together.'

'Yes. That, I like.'

She stepped back and he followed her inside.

'Oh.' He blinked as he entered the living room, identical in size and shape to his, but bedecked with winter foliage and twinkling lights. Like something from a shopfront, television, or one of the glossy magazines he'd seen in Georgia's house. 'I guess this is not good for you.'

'Not really.'

Farid lifted a reindeer cushion from the sofa. 'Cute, no?'

She cocked her head with another slaying look.

'It's a nice cushion.' He stroked the deer. 'And cuddly too.'

'It's horrible if you ask me.'

'You worry about the strangest things. You don't like the elf and my red hat or this sweet little cushion.'

'Oh jeez. I'm sorry. You're right. It's silly when you put it like that.'

'It's ok.'

'No, it isn't.' She slumped onto the sofa and picked up one of the red tartan cushions, holding it close to her chest. 'Sit down.' Tilting her head, she indicated he should take the space next to her.

Over familiar, much? They'd just met an hour ago but smouldering flames whipped him forward. Warmth seeped into every pore as he sank down beside her.

'Tell me about yourself.'

He wove his fingers together. 'Nothing to say. I am what you see.'

'Your English is very good.'

'I learned at school and my father worked in oil. He talked to the British and Americans a lot. I picked things up and when I start working, I use it sometimes too.'

'Georgia said that's why you came here. Your father knew Archie.'

'Yes. My father had connections. I was lucky.'

'Why did you leave?'

'I was in a group that challenged the government. They captured and tortured us. We escaped. It wasn't safe to stay after that.'

She stretched out her hand and placed it on his knee. The sting of attraction shot up his thigh and into his groin. She was fast. He inhaled, accepting the touch. As well as the burn, it brought comfort.

'I can't begin to comprehend it. How dreadful. It makes my worries seem utterly stupid.' She squeezed his knee and he put his hand over hers. *Stop. Stop.* His sanity depended on it. Or at least his control.

'You must have reasons.'

She looked him in the eye. He held his breath. Those lips begged to be kissed. He could dip in and claim the first true kiss of his life. *Must not move. Don't do it. Stay still.*

'I do. But they're ridiculous when I hear what you've been through.' Her other hand landed on top of his, sandwiching him between her beautifully soft palms.

His lungs spasmed. *Breathe. Stay cool.* But how? '*Ya'ni*, I won't forget, but I must think about the future. Going back is not something I can do.'

'That's a great mindset. You must be resilient.' She rested her head on the back of the sofa close to his shoulder, still not moving her gaze from him. 'How about we eat some pies and drown our sorrows? I have wine.'

'I didn't drink much before I arrived here but I like the sound of it.'

'I can tell you're my kind of guy.'

A tremor rippled through him. She was definitely his kind of woman. No one had ever set his blood racing like this.

'I have a condition.' Farid edged his face a fraction closer. One centimetre more and the tips of their noses would touch.

'What? Like hives or something? Should I keep my distance?'

He frowned. 'You joke, huh? But no, not like that.'

Her lip curled. 'Yeah, I'm joking.' She ran her thumb over a raised vein on the back of his hand and he tightened his grip. Her deep eye contact scorched him low. 'Tell me your condition then.'

'You stay. Don't go yet.'

'That's it?'

'Yes. I help you.'

'How the hell will you do that?'

'Magic.' He winked.

Holly gazed at him for a few seconds. 'You're cute.' Lifting her hand from his, she tapped the end of his nose with her index finger and he chuckled. 'Quite a bit more than cute. Tell you what. Let's eat. If I like the pies, I might stay.'

'You make a hard bargain.'

'You have no idea.' She raised her eyebrows and got to her feet. He followed.

'You like music?' he asked.

'As long as it's not some Christmas thing, then yes.'

'Let's see what I find.' He turned up the volume on the radio and a song he didn't recognise played out. It sounded like a children's choir. He glanced at Holly. 'What is this one?'

She screwed up her nose. 'It's called "War is Over".'

'Then, it sounds perfect.'

'It's a Christmas song.' She made her way to the small kitchen area at the end of the living area. An L-shaped unit doubled as a breakfast bar and dining table and divided the two areas.

'I change it,' he said. 'But, for sure, I do not get the connection to war and Christmas.'

'Seriously, Farid, no one knows what Christmas is about anymore. That's part of the problem. It takes up such a huge percentage of every year. People waste so much time and energy on it and businesses cash in left, right and centre. But it's pointless. Unless you're making money from it, it's a brain drain, a cash drain and a soul crusher.'

'Oh, Holly, Holly.' He changed the channel. Classical vibes played and he glanced at her. 'Is this ok?'

'It'll do. At least it has nothing to do with reindeer, bells, Santa or bloody gingerbread.'

He snorted. 'You like me to light the fire for you?'

'Knock yourself out.'

'You want me to knock myself out first? With this?' He picked up a log, pretending to bash the side of his head with it.

'It's just a figure of speech. It means yes please.'

'I worked that out.' He stacked logs on the fire and built up the kindling. 'It will get hot in here later.'

'It's quite hot already.'

Farid grinned and strolled into the kitchen behind her. The urge to wrap his arms around her from behind was powerful. Would she like that? *Too fast. Way too fast.* His hot blood was pushing him into all kinds of crazy. 'I find Christmas very confusing,' he said.

'You and me both. But for now, we'll stick to basics.' She turned around and stopped dead. A smile played on her lips and she eyed him up.

'And they are?'

'Mince pies, booze and staying off the naughty list.' She lifted a bottle of wine from the work surface and waggled it.

'What is the naughty list?'

'I'll explain later, but right now, my name is very close to being on it. Time to behave and see what I make of your pies.' She tipped him a wink.

He took the bottle from her, moving closer. 'I think you'll like them.'

'Ooh.' She quirked her eyebrow. 'Let's have them then.'

'And don't forget, you like, you stay.'

She smiled, lifted the box of pies and handed it to Farid. 'So, what do we do with these?'

Right now? Throw them in the bin and grab her instead. Whoa. Protocols here might be more relaxed than he was used to, but a move like that and she might slap him and turf him out. Rightly so. He took the pies and switched on the oven. Her eyes burned through him, watching every move.

His hand shook slightly as he took out a tray. What was he doing? If she liked his food, what else might she like? He twiddled his fingers, eyeing the pies through the oven door.

Holly opened and closed three cupboard doors. 'Aha.' She pulled two enormous wine glasses and placed them on the work-top, then popped the cork on the wine bottle. Blood red liquid swirled into them.

'Cheers.' She passed him a glass and clinked hers against his.

'*Fe Sehetak.*' He took a sip and blinked. 'Strong, huh?'

'Strong and deep. As I like my men.' She waggled her eye-brows.

'Ah. This is why you are on the naughty list.'

She chuckled, and it brought a sparkle to her eyes, lighting her face.

Farid downed a large slug of wine, grabbed a dishcloth and pulled out the tray of steaming pies.

Holly topped up her glass, shaking the dregs from the bottle. 'Just as well I got two.' She flapped away a yawn. 'All the travel-ling. It's tired me out. Let's be even more naughty and eat on the sofa. I need a comfy seat.' Lifting her glass and a fresh bottle, she ported them across the room and laid them on the coffee table. Farid dished the pies onto plates and slid them over the worktop. Holly took them to the table, then flopped onto the sofa.

'Now we see if you stay or go.' Farid sipped his wine, then sat beside her.

'Ok.' She picked up a plate, balancing it close to her mouth as she bit into the pie. Her head rocked from side to side as she chewed.

'Well?'

'Good, really nice actually.'

'You like?'

'I do.'

'That means you stay.'

She took another bite and nodded. 'Ok.'

'Tell me how you know Georgia.' Farid lifted his own plate.

'We shared a flat at uni. We were on different courses but we got thrown together as housemates and hit it off.'

Farid leaned his elbow on the back of the sofa, facing her as she spoke. Watching her eyes dance as she talked warmed his heart.

When she finished her pie, she topped up her glass again and knocked it back. 'This is good stuff.' She admired her glass. 'Here. Let's have a toast. To new neighbours.'

Farid raised an eyebrow as she clinked her glass on the side of his. 'Why do you want to give me toast?'

She lowered her glass and covered her mouth. 'Oh god, that's hilarious. Not that kind of toast. Oh, jeez. This country makes no sense, does it?'

'Not often.'

'I'll explain.'

The sound of her voice brought a smile to his lips. He leaned his chin on his hand. She finished her wine and slapped the glass on the table, yawning again.

'Sorry, I'm so...' She flapped her hand in front of her face. 'Tired.' Her head dropped back and she stared at the ceiling. 'It's so warm in here.'

'Let me clear up.' Farid took the plates and glasses into the kitchen area and loaded them into the compact dishwasher. When he got back to the living area, Holly's head drooped to the side. For a second, Farid eyed the gentle movement of her chest rising and falling, then he picked up a blanket from a wire basket in the corner and threw it over her.

'Goodnight.' One last glance and he let himself out into the cold evening air. He wasn't alone on this little outpost anymore. Through the wall was a woman who'd rocked his mind in a few short hours.

Chapter Six

Holly

As mornings after went, this was ok. A little too much wine had been consumed the night before. Coupled with the travelling, it had made Holly so tired she'd fallen asleep on the sofa in front of the fire. When she'd woken, someone had put a blanket over her.

Must have been Farid. She rubbed the dull ache on her forehead. 'Shit and double shit.' Had she blown it? Whatever 'it' was. It wasn't like she had a game plan. The last thing she would have expected was to be holed up beside the most handsome guy in the universe... Apart from the overload of Christmas décor. Where that was an unwelcome surprise, Farid definitely wasn't.

She showered and dressed, then found herself at the kitchen window, leaning on the sink, gazing out to sea. The sky was blue and clear but the sea was wild. Wind whipped across its surface. Holly pulled open the dishwasher. Shiny plates and glasses sparkled at her. Farid had cleared up. Seriously? Could he be any more of a gentleman? And she liked his pies – that meant two things. First, he was a good cook and second, she'd promised to stay for a bit longer. But something had to be done about this cottage first. The Christmas stuff was cringy. She pulled a cup from the washer and stopped, holding it suspended in mid-air. Running up the steep track from the beach some hundred feet below was Farid. Hot. Hot. Hot. Middle of winter, yes, but a cold shower was in order right now. He was in shorts, and his legs. Oh no. Not his legs too. They were strong, covered in dark hair and altogether the shapeliest man legs possible.

He stopped at the top, leaned over and rested his palms on his knees, panting. When he straightened up, he loosened the neck of his t-shirt and shook his curly head. Holly scooted back from the window. *Don't want him to catch me drooling.* What the hell would he think? What did he think anyway? She was some lightweight who couldn't hold her drink? Couldn't have that. Ditching the cup, she nipped to the front door and wrenched it open. Her breath billowed in front of her.

'Hey.' She cupped her hand around her mouth. The distant rush of the waves and the rustle of the wind in the grass were the only other sounds.

Farid stopped at the end of the little patch of green before the house. Such a barren garden.

He leaned on the gate. 'Hi. You woke up then?'

Folding her arms, she strutted towards him. Slippers be damned. He wasn't leaving that gate until she'd made her point. 'It must have been the travelling. I hardly ever do that. Or you drugged the pies.'

'No, not me.' He pulled an innocent face.

She cocked her head. 'And thanks for clearing up.'

'It's nothing. Christmas spirit and all that.'

'Seriously? Washing dishes is Christmassy now, is it?'

'Everything is Christmassy in this crazy country. You should be Christmassy. You are Holly. I see holly in every display.' He threw out his hands. 'But does anyone know why?'

'Search me.'

His eyes obeyed, roaming over her. A shiver coursed through her and she hugged herself. 'It's another figure of speech.'

'No?' He flashed an ironic look.

'I've no idea why I'm called Holly. My birthday's in September, so it was nothing to do with Christmas.'

He pulled up his eyebrows. 'No?'

'No.'

'Maybe your parents found a Christmas connection. *Ya'ni*, like the Christmas nine months before you were born.'

'Oh, Jesus Christ.' She slapped her palm into her forehead. 'That's an image I really don't need.' Though possibly, most annoyingly, he was right.

He laughed, turning her insides to liquid. 'You cried the name Jesus Christ. That is definitely Christmassy, yes.'

'Obviously. But does anyone celebrate Christmas because of that anymore?' She held out her hands. 'If that's the true meaning of Christmas, then it's lost.'

'Sad.' Farid tipped his head to the side, the corners of his lips drooping.

'Why are you so interested in Christmas anyway?'

'Because it's everywhere here. It's huge. But it makes no sense.' He rubbed his arms and shivered. 'I'm freezing. I stand still too long. I must shower.'

Holly arched an eyebrow. That would be fun to watch... or join.

He winked.

Had he read her mind? She remained in the garden as he opened his gate and drew level with her on the other side of the fence.

'So, you stay, then?'

'For a little while.'

His smile spread over his well-proportioned face, dimpling his cheeks. 'Good. I make you some more food. I hear sprouts are popular this time of year.'

'Oh, bugger off.' She pushed his shoulder and he reeled back, laughing. With another cheeky wink, he hopped inside and shut the door.

Holly raked up her hair, lifting it high off her head and letting it float back down. What a tease. A delicious, sexy tease, but there was more to him than that. Through his cheer, she sensed a lingering sadness. He was alone here and needed a friend. That she could do. Easy. She returned to her own house. Time to work. But unholy thoughts of him showering next door were distracting.

'I knew this would happen.' She rapped her finger on the edge of her laptop. 'He's far too bloody gorgeous for his own good. And mine.' Plus the lonely vibes he gave off resonated a bit too keenly. Lonely people always felt worse at Christmas – apparently. Maybe the festive effect was subconsciously filtering in, highlighting insecurities that didn't normally bother her.

The breakfast bar-cum-table was the closest Holly had to a desk. She sat with her back to the living room to avoid having to view *The Nightmare Before Christmas*.

She composed an email to her prospective new client before she started working on her ongoing jobs. The Wi-Fi was acceptable, just as well because mobile phone signal was non-existent on this part of the island. A reply pinged in from her client and she read through it, her eyes narrowing. So much for their lucrative offer. This could turn sour very quickly. The job appeared interesting and challenging but a name flashed like a warning beacon. Gavin Sinclair. He was on the team of developers she'd be working with. Her blood cooled. What an unwelcome ghost from Christmas past.

'Screw it.' She threw her head into her hands. Would she never be free from him? They'd been at uni together, studied together, worked in the same field, dated, and so much more. For a while, he'd been her everything. And with him being in the same line as her, it was impossible to avoid him cropping up. She hunched over her laptop. Would the Gavin shitstorm ever blow over? Cold contact via emails was as much as she could handle. But working in a team with him? No. She shuddered like the Christmas tat was creeping up from behind ready to pounce on her. Or maybe it was him in his Christmas jumper, grabbing her and dangling mistletoe over her head, kissing her cheek and laughing, as he'd done on Christmas morning. *The* Christmas morning of *that* day.

With a sharp click, Holly minimised the email. This required thought. Working remotely would mean no face-to-face contact, but even calls could be tense. *Ugh.*

A message head popped up on her phone. A grinning face with large sunglasses filled the bubble. Her sister Alice.

ALICE: Where are you? You've gone AWOL again. Mum went round to your flat and says it looks deserted. We've called and called but it's ringing out. I hope you're ok! X

Holly pulled a side-pout. Oops. She'd 'forgotten', ahem, to tell her family what she was doing. Not that they needed to know urgently. Her last flat was in a pleasant part of Stirling and her parents lived miles away in the borders. After her father had retired from his job in the defence industry, they'd settled for the first time in years. If her mother had *called round* it was a fluke rather than design. Holly and Alice's childhood had been nomadic. They'd rarely lived anywhere for over two or three years. Alice had moved to Wolverhampton when she got married and Holly occasionally drove south to meet her. But not at Christmas... Well, not since the Gavin Christmas.

She typed a quick reply.

ME: Sorry, I forgot to say. I moved out of the flat a few days ago. I'm living in a friend's cottage on the Isle of Mull for a while. Not sure how long. I'll catch up with everyone in the new year. Mobile reception is rubbish here but I'll drive into Tobermory at some point and send a message to Mum. Unless you can get her to sign up to a messenger that uses Wi-Fi.

Not a chance. But she put it in anyway. As she hit send, the neighbouring door clunked shut. Was that Farid off to work? Her toes twitched, ready to leap across the room so she could look out the front window to see him driving off. Sighing, she stared at her screen. Living here was going to be a bitch. But for now, he was gone. Work called. She pottered away at her jobs, getting up every now and again to make a coffee. Georgia had left a Christmas hot chocolate selection box in the cupboard. 'Is someone trying to make me leave?' Holly flicked the switch on the kettle. Beyond the window, the tufty grass blew in the wind. A boat sailed serenely up the channel beyond.

The washer vibrated loudly. With a wind like that, she could risk hanging it up outside. Better than wet stuff hanging around the house when space for an airer was non-existent. Two steps into the garden and she was almost blown off her feet. Sharp gusts stung her cheeks and she battled around the gable end. A whirligig leaned precariously to one side. She started pegging out the clothes. As she pegged up a pair of burgundy lace knickers, a pickup pulled up at the front gate. Great timing. Farid was back already. Right on cue to see her hanging up her undies.

He jumped out and was about to go in his own gate when he glanced up and their eyes met. She waved from behind a flapping towel. He strolled over, raking his fingers through those glorious curls. Did he have to do that? He was handsome enough without having to rub it in.

'How can I help you?' She pegged up the last item. Farid tugged at the collar of his lumberjack shirt. How hot did he look? 'Have you made some more pies? Or do you want to pull my Christmas cracker?'

His lip curled up. 'I'm not sure what that is. It sounds both naughty and nice.'

'Very seasonal then.'

'I just come to say hi because you wave.'

'Oh, my fault, is it?'

'*Ay*, your fault. But you are still here. You hang out clothes, so you must be staying a bit, no?'

She folded her arms. 'Well, that's my forfeit for liking your cooking.'

'*Ay*, that's it.' He held up his finger. 'I can persuade you with my food.'

She arched an eyebrow. Right now, she didn't need food. One smile from those lips and she'd do anything. 'I thought I'd give it a whirl. See how I get on for a day or two.'

'Oh. Look.' He pointed to the sea. 'Three boats. I think that's a sign.'

'What?' She turned and shielded her eyes from the wind and the glare. Where she'd seen the boat shortly before, there were now three sailing in a row. A sign? More like another festive poke in the ribs. 'It's like that bloody Christmas song, "I Saw Three Ships". And really, that proves what I was telling you before, because what in hell's name have ships to do with Christmas?'

Farid threw out his hands. 'You tell me. Maybe they bring three things. Wait one second...' He took out his phone and scrolled through it. 'Here, I use translate. Maybe a sign of peace, prosperity and love.'

'Seriously? Quite the romantic, aren't you?'

'Maybe. I like peace and love. These things I miss.'

Holly dropped her head to the side. 'You miss your family?'

'Of course. My family are everything. And now, I may not see them again. Not for a long time. But now, I'm here and this is where I will grow. Put the roots in the ground and make this my home.'

'You're planning on staying here?' Holly picked up the collapsible washing basket and flattened it.

'Sure.' Farid fell into step with her, strolling towards the house. She was pushing five foot ten. He was a couple of inches taller and broad shouldered.

'Why? I never find enough in one place to keep me. I'm not sure why anyone would want to be tied down.' Memories of days with Gavin swam to the surface again. Yup, there had been a time in her life when that was what she dreamed of. She blinked the thoughts away.

'*Ya'ni,* I see those boats and I wonder where they go, who is on them and why? I remember how I get here. I travel through many hostile places, see horrible things, do things I'm not proud of.'

'Oh?'

'*Ay,* I pay big money to get out of Syria on a boat that really I shouldn't. I hide in trucks to get over borders. I beg on the streets. These things, they are not me. So, now, I'm here. I don't want to do that again. I want to be home. And so I have to make this my home.'

She nodded. 'When you put it like that, it makes sense.'

'Holly, I will teach you something.'

'You will?' She eyed him over. This sounded promising.

'*Ay,* I will teach you the magic of being home.'

'Oh-kay.' The word came out slowly, covering her scepticism in two syllables.

His bright blue eyes glinted from beneath his dark brows, begging her to come closer. 'But I don't give my lessons for free. You must give me something in return.'

Was that a pick-up line? Christ, he was crazy gorgeous, heart-palpitation-inducing attractive, but she wasn't sticking around. A fling was fine and good. Nothing else. She didn't do long-term. Whatever he was going to suggest, she wanted that to be crystal clear. Any dates she had these days came with disclaimers so everyone was on the same page. No chance of big feel-ings. Her heart was her own, not something to be carved up like a turkey on Christmas Day and shared around. But warning bells sounded louder than the jingling ones on Santa's sleigh. Farid had the power to do serious damage. Even from their miniscule acquaintance, it was apparent. 'So what's your price? Because I like to get my money's worth.'

'I can tell.' His teeth glinted as he grinned. 'I teach you about the magic of home. You teach me about the magic of Christmas.'

'No way.' She stomped to the front door. 'Why do you want to know about that? It's consumerist crap, that's what it is. I'd have thought you'd know better.'

'*La, la, la.*' He waggled his finger. 'It is money, yes. Everything is money and something this big will make money. People would be crazy not to use it. What I want you to teach me is the magic.'

'I know nothing about that.'

'Don't know or you forget?'

'Both, probably.'

'Then let's find it together.' Farid took her hand and squeezed it gently, sending pleasure bolts into her bloodstream. 'Let's make magic.'

Holly bit into her lip. What was his game? Was he a tease? Or was this something he genuinely wanted? Why not dispense with the games and go straight to making magic? Or she could humour him. How hard would it be to make him a hot choco-late, give him a gingerbread house to decorate and let him cuddle a fluffy penguin? Once that was done and dusted, she could substitute the penguin for herself and let the real magic begin. Easy as pie – mince pies, no less. She returned the pressure on his hand. 'Ok, it's a deal.'

His grin was back. He let go of her hand and gave her the thumbs up. 'I must grab lunch. I forget to lift it when I leave. Then I go back to work. But lessons start soon.' He winked and tapped her arm. 'And I won't forget.'

Holly nipped into the house and slumped onto the sofa opposite the Christmas tree.

'I thought I had a perfectly normal and well-planned life,' she told the gleaming silver baubles. She'd believed that before. Six Christmases ago. She was skating on the tip of an iceberg again. *Just don't fall off the edge into chaos this time.*

Chapter Seven

Farid

Farid grinned at Georgia's little shop, The Boat Shack. Constructed like an upturned boat, it was both quirky and appealing. And so fitting with the sea backdrop. Inside, she and her friend, Autumn, had decked it out beautifully with handmade artisan products. Farid browsed their latest creations, lifting candles to his nostrils and inhaling the perfect blends. Sea breeze aromas mingled with something spicier and warmer.

He picked up a toffee coloured one in a jar labelled Gingerbread Hugs, then a dark navy one with glitter throughout named Starry Night. Finally, a rich brown one with a white top: Christmas Cake. Something about this one called to him.

'What is in this?' he said. 'I love it.'

Both Georgia and Autumn looked around. Neither woman was tall, but both had smiles to light up dark places. Autumn tossed a mane of red hair over her shoulder. 'It's a bit of a trade secret, but it's mainly citrus, mixed spice and almond, to give a hint of marzipan.'

'*Ya'ni*, it smells beautiful. I would like to make a Christmas cake.'

'They're complicated.' Georgia aligned a snow scene canvas on the wall. Real lights twinkled magically from it, like starlight through trees. 'You have to leave them to stew for several weeks.'

'Like a Christmas pudding.' Autumn placed a candle on a glass shelf and stepped back. 'But there's still time. Just don't leave it much later.'

'I might need some help.'

'I could try,' Georgia said. 'But I'm not great at baking and I'm really busy.'

'I'll ask my neighbour.' Farid took another sniff of the candle.

'Oh, my god, no.' Georgia held up her hands. 'I don't think she's speaking to me after the decorations. She hates Christmas.'

'Ah, we'll see.' Farid tipped his head. 'I'm working on her.'

Georgia's eyebrows raised into the strands of the tousled bob covering her forehead. She cast a brief glance at Autumn.

'What?' Farid threw up his palms, pulling an innocent face.

'I dread to think.'

'Nothing to dread. All good.'

Georgia chuckled, returning to the shelves and adding some wintery prints to a box.

'Can I see the grotto?' Farid said. 'I wonder always what a grotto is.'

'Sure. Just go in. I'm not sure why it's called that. It's a place where kids can meet Santa and get a present.'

'One of these traditions no one understands.' The list was getting longer every second.

'I guess. Christmas started two thousand years ago with the birth of Christ. But before that, there were pagan festivals, Yule, Saturnalia and midwinter. All these have been absorbed into Christmas over the centuries and other things keep being added on. Every family has their own traditions peculiar to them.'

'It's confusing when I haven't grown up knowing them.'

'You can make your own too,' Autumn said. 'My husband, Richard, is an atheist and doesn't really care about Christmas, but I enjoy it, so we've decided to make our own traditions. We've drawn on Christmassy inspired ideas but we're making them into what we want and what suits us.'

'Exactly,' Georgia said. 'It's like Australians and Kiwis who want the traditional Christmas lunch. They roast turkeys on the barbecue and have beach parties wearing swimming costumes and Santa hats.'

Farid clapped his hands and smirked. 'Not sure you've made it easier to understand or worse. What a lot to remember. But thank you. I look at the grotto, then go. Your logs are out front.'

'Thanks, Farid,' Georgia said. 'If you want to come back on Saturday, Santa will be here. You can sit on his knee and get a pencil set.'

He facepalmed. 'How very strange.'

Georgia and Autumn chuckled.

Farid left, making his way around the back. A man with long blond dreadlocks was up a ladder, hammering a curtain into a beam. 'Hello, Blair,' Farid said. He'd met the joiner on several occasions now. What an amazing talent he had. He'd constructed this wooden shed behind the boat shop in less than a day.

'Hi,' Blair said. 'How are you?'

'Good. Do you need help with that?'

'It's cool, thanks, I'm nearly done.'

'I came to look around. It's very interesting.' In the corner was a large wooden chair and on one wall was a fake, but convincing, fireplace. Bags of decorations littered the floor, including the one with the offensive elf costume he'd thrust at Holly the day she'd arrived.

'It'll look better once Georgia and Autumn have decorated it. I'm just finishing this bit, then I'm off. Rebekah and I are going Christmas shopping.' He jumped off the ladder and rolled his eyes. 'I've obviously not done it properly every other year. I just picked up bits and bobs but she wants an afternoon in Oban.'

Farid winked. 'You do it then. Keep the ladies happy.'

'Absolutely.' Blair dusted his hands together. 'And I can drop some hints if I see anything I like.'

'Good thinking.'

Back in the pickup, Farid drove to the wooded area of the estate where he was clearing the dead wood and selective felling the Sitka and Norway spruces. Smaller and less prickly ones might be neat Christmas trees but Archie wanted them off the land to maintain the ancient woodland on the estate. Blair's father, Mike, was helping with the work along with local forester, Per Hansen. Farid jumped out of the pickup and grabbed his hard hat.

He let out a long, slow exhale, gazing into the distance, focusing on nothing. Both these guys were experienced in the trade, settled and confident. Farid was scrabbling uphill, learning new skills in an industry he knew little about.

He dragged the tools from the back of the pickup, shoulders drooped and his heart heavy.

'Everything ok?' Per asked as Farid approached.

He nodded. '*Ay.*'

'Carl's dropping by shortly for some offcuts; I thought it was him when I heard the pickup.'

'No. Just me.'

Per checked up from his clipboard and smiled.

Carl was Per's youngest son. The warmth in his voice when he spoke of his three grown-up children and grandchildren struck Farid square in the chest. Back home, he had family connections. Generations working and living close by: his father doling out advice – whether or not he wanted to hear it; his mother feeding him up and talking non-stop about everyone else's business; his sisters squabbling over what to wear or closeted somewhere watching YouTube videos on how to style hair and paint nails.

Working with these men hammered it home. Each night they went back to their families, while he went home alone.

'I delivered the logs,' Farid said. 'You tell me what to do next.' They guided him. Best way. He was little more than a labourer. His training and experience weren't in this field. But work was work.

'We'll fell this one next.' Per scanned a fir from root to tip. 'We need to minimise the impact on the vegetation, so let's make sure she falls that way.'

'Yes.' Farid stalked around the tree, skimming up, then down and calculating the angles. 'So, work from here.' He stopped at the spot and pointed forward. 'Should I work out the trajectory?'

Mike placed his hands on his hips and laughed. 'I don't even know what that means and I've been cutting trees for over twenty years.'

'He's quite right.' Per's glasses balanced on the tip of his nose as he made notes on his clipboard. 'We should work it out. When you've done it as long as us, it becomes second nature, that's all. But even we make mistakes. So, yes, measure it out, please.'

'Sure,' Farid said. 'I have a mathematical background, not trees, so I do what comes naturally.'

'What did you do before?' Mike dragged his chainsaw box out of the way.

'Computer programming.' Farid pulled out his phone, ready to key in the numbers.

'Really?' Per said. 'You're a quick learner then. I thought you had forestry experience and that's why you got this job.'

'No. I can't apply for programming jobs. My qualifications don't work here.'

'But surely that doesn't matter if you can do the job. Aren't computer codes the same everywhere? Or is that me showing my ignorance?'

'They follow the same principle. But I will struggle to get a job without the right qualifications. I was lucky to know Archie. He offers me this and I take it. I was desperate. And now I start, it's not so bad.'

'You're doing a good job,' Per said. 'You could get a qualification in this if you wanted, but it seems a waste if you're already qualified for something else.'

'It won't be easy to get a job in this country doing computing. Before I got my refugee status, I wasn't permitted to work. Asylum seekers cannot get jobs here. After, I tried, but I had nowhere to live. I slept rough for some weeks. None of it is good when applying for work. I don't even have a computer now. Only a phone. So I stick with this job.'

'Dear me, lad.' Per clapped him on the shoulder. 'You've had a terrible ride.'

'*Ya'ni.*' Farid thrust his hands into his pockets. 'Don't worry about it. I'm here now.'

'You are. And I'm glad you're safe.'

'Thank you.'

They set to work putting the markers in place. Farid made the calculations. Mike powered up the saw and before long, the interloping spruce keeled to the ground, leaving the indigenous woodland to breathe again. While Mike trimmed off the branches and cut the trunk into manageable sections, Per and Farid trudged deeper into the wood. Per examined the trees, marking a couple with spray paint that were to come down next.

'Do you have family?' he asked Farid as he waded through the straggly undergrowth.

'Parents, yes, and two sisters. Other family too, but no wife and no children.'

'You're a young man; there's no rush.'

'It might be a long time before I can go back. Maybe never.'

'You might meet someone here.'

Holly jumped to the forefront, waving in his face, ever present, like a brain worm gnawing away at him. Nothing would fully shake her from his mind. 'I suppose I might. I just don't know if it's quite right.'

'It's the modern world, Farid.' Per slashed an X onto a tree trunk with his paint spray. 'People are people all over the world. You're allowed to date someone here if you want to.'

In principle, he didn't mind the idea. 'I just wonder what my family will think. What if I meet someone and they can never see her? It's so difficult.'

'Yes. I get what you mean. That's not easy. My two older boys are married to Americans and even that can be hard sometimes, sharing between the families, so what you're up against is much worse. But don't feel lonely. If you want company, call around the house. It's called Tighnatraigh and it's just outside Salen, a mile up from the Glen Lodge Hotel, call in any time. My wife and I will be thrilled to have you.'

'Thank you, that's very kind.'

Per patted him on the back and warm, fatherly affection flowed from the older man's hand. No one could replace his father, but Per could join the rank of uncle. Farid's fondness for his colleague burned strong, refreshing his sense of purpose.

Darkness closed around them as the afternoon drew on. 'We'll call it a day,' Per said as they shared the logs into their vehicles. 'We can't do much else without daylight.'

Days were short in the winter and Farid looked forward to the promise of long days in the summer. In midsummer, according to Georgia, there were barely three hours of dark and even during those hours, you could see clearly. How magical. In Syria, there were long nights in December but even in summer, the sun set by eight, closing hot days with cool evenings.

Farid drove back to the cottage. When he arrived, pitch black had descended. The lights on Holly's side of the building glowed, warm and welcoming. Farid jumped out of the pickup. Stars dotted the sky, twinkling like a net of gems. Cold air nipped. How like the starry night candle he'd sniffed that morning. He kept his eyes skyward, finding familiar constellations. Even though he was so far from home, the skies were constant. Perhaps his mother and sisters were looking up at the same stars. The thought wrapped around him like a warm blanket, giving him hope. *I wish I could see your faces and give you a hug. I love you.*

A door clicked and Farid rolled his neck, peering toward the house. Holly was silhouetted in her doorframe.

'Is that you, Farid?' she called.

'Yes, me. Are you ok?'

'I'm fine. Well, I'm freezing but I heard a car drawing up, then no one came to the door and I didn't hear your door, so I wondered what was going on.'

'I'm stargazing. You should too. Come see.'

'I'm not exactly dressed for it. It's so cold outside. Hang on. Let me grab a coat and some shoes.'

Farid rubbed his hands together and blew on them. Moments later, Holly's gate creaked, and she sidled up beside him.

'What am I to look at?'

'Just this. It's like a thousand diamonds.'

She glanced up and cocked her head. 'Wow. There's no orange light to pollute it. It's beautiful.'

Just like you. Farid kept the thought firmly inside.

'Back home, we have the same stars. Maybe my family look at them right now too.'

'Is Syria in the same time zone as the UK?'

'Three hours ahead. But my family are in Turkey now. Two hours ahead. So, it's about seven o'clock there.'

'Maybe they're looking too then.'

'I hope so.'

Holly curled her arm behind his back and clamped her hand on his shoulder, giving him a stoic pat. 'You're a brave man. You've been through tough times.'

'Yes.'

'Your body's done the hard work but now it's a struggle for the heart and mind.'

'You say wise words. How do you know?' He shifted so his temple touched hers.

'I don't for sure. It just seems to me that's what's happening. I've had hard times in my life too. Nothing like what you've been through but enough for me to understand.'

'It's not a competition. Your hard times are as real as mine. Only different.' He slipped his arm under hers, anchoring his palm on her waist and holding her tight. How gloriously athletic in build, slim and strong. And so good in his arms. *Don't let go. Don't ever let go.* She shivered and he drew her closer. Just a few months ago, he'd slept under harsh skies in unfriendly streets. Cold and alone with a cracked heart and tears never far from the surface. Now, he had a chance to make good again. And Holly. What an unexpected bonus to have her next door.

'It's freezing out here.' She gave his shoulder a squeeze. 'I should go in. I'm not dressed for this.'

'What are you wearing?' He quirked an eyebrow, shifting his hand slightly and touching the fabric of her coat, searching for clues.

'Not a lot. I've been faffing around in my jammies all day. The cottage is really warm when the fire's on.'

'Sounds nice. I must warm up now; my hands are frozen.' The luxury of having a home to return to: warmth, shelter and food. Not so good as his parents' place he'd left in Daraa but better than a cold pavement or a shop doorway.

'Come in with me if you like. I'll even let you share my gourmet pasta tea.'

'Would you?'

'Of course. I owe you after the pies.'

'No, no. All you owe me is to stay here.'

'Yeah, yeah, and I'm doing that. Come on, let's get you warmed up.'

How could he refuse? For months his heart had craved soft words like that, promising comfort. She took his hand and tugged on it but she didn't have to. He was already following.

Inside her front door, she shrugged off her coat and hung it on a hook. Farid took hold of the top button of his lumberjack shirt, ready to do the same, but did a double take. Oh god. What was she wearing – or not wearing? She kicked off her outdoor boots, revealing perfectly pedicured bare feet. His gaze travelled upwards over black and grey checked lounge pants, low slung on strong hips. On top was a plain white vest top. What ridiculously flimsy material; it should be banned for such clothes. It hid noth-ing – two peaks raised beneath it, targeting Farid in the groin. He blinked back a succession of jumbled images. Ones of him rubbing scented oil on his palms and gliding them over her were most prominent. *Shit.*

A cardigan of the same fabric draped low on her shoulders and swung down behind her. Curse his eyes but he couldn't drag them from her perfectly shaped chest quick enough. His body burst into flames; a wild animal clawed within desperate for a mate. He let out a slow breath that came out like a groan.

'Problem?' Holly barely concealed a smirk. She slid her cardigan up her shoulder, toying with the fabric between her fingertips. Farid closed his mouth and swallowed.

'Eh? *Ya'ni,* nothing. No. All good.' He hauled off his jacket, exposing his deeply tanned arms. Now, it was her turn to stare, and she didn't disguise her blatant once over. She raised a shapely eyebrow and one side of her mouth quirked up. Farid tossed back his shoulders.

Holly ran a finger down his arm and he almost jumped out of his skin. 'You're a mighty fine-looking man.'

Heat bloomed in his cheeks. 'Oh.' Was that all he could say? Curse his slow tongue. Where were the words? His inexperience with women shone like a beacon.

'No point in denying it. Now, come through and we'll put on some food.'

He followed her into the heat of the living room. 'Wow.' He tugged at his neckline. 'It's hot.' Everything in the room was setting him ablaze. Holly's gaze seared him with an unquenchable desire, but palpations erupted in his chest. What was he meant to

do here? He was playing with fire. Being burned would follow…
But how? Good burn or bad burn?

'It just got hotter,' she muttered. 'Now.' She clapped her hands before he could speak. 'While you're here, would you like your first lesson about Christmas?'

'Er… I'm not sure.'

If she plucked out a whip and cracked it on the breakfast bar in front of him, he wouldn't be surprised. 'Partridges and pear trees.'

'What?'

'Yes. It's from the song "The Twelve Days of Christmas". It's one of the bizarre songs we churn out this time of year. It goes through the twelve days and each day there's a more extravagant gift starting with a partridge in a pear tree and ending with twelve lords-a-leaping.'

'And what is it to do with Christmas?'

Holly threw out her palms. 'Not a clue. Every year we used to sing it at school and each row in the assembly hall was assigned a line and we had to stand up when it was our line. It's scarred me for life. I can't hear that song without panicking I'll forget to stand up when seven swans are swimming.'

Farid rubbed his forehead. 'I am so lost with this.'

'Well, that makes two of us.'

'And this is why you hate Christmas?'

'No.' She dug a corkscrew into a bottle of wine. 'It's much more complicated than that. Tell you what, let's get sloshed and

I'll teach you the lyrics. Then we can stand up and sit down at our turn and see if either of us can stand up after five gold rings.'

Farid buried his head in his hands and laughed. 'I have no idea what you are talking about.'

A glass hit the table in front of him. He picked it up and Holly held hers out. They clinked. Her eyes burned into his. What should he do now? Make a move? What move?

'*Sláinte.*' She winked. He'd heard that word used since arriving in Scotland but coming from Holly's lips, it seemed more of a promise than a salute.

'*Fe Sehetak.*' He raised his glass and knocked back a mouthful.

A shrewd expression swept over Holly's face. Farid held his breath.

'Let's get this pasta cooking,' she said. 'Then I can tell you about my two front teeth.'

'Your what?'

She giggled as she pulled out a pan and filled it with water. 'You did say you wanted to learn.'

'I think you're making things up to confuse me.'

'Nope. I promise I'm not.' She waggled her eyebrows and he shook his head. Right now, she could tell him Christmas involved skinny dipping in the icy ocean on live TV and he would do it. He was putty and however she wanted him, he would bend.

Chapter Eight

Holly

A deep musk tingled in Holly's nostrils as flames flickered from the candles on the worktop dining table. Her eyes locked on Farid while they ate. Words weren't necessary. Their gazes communicated. A taut wire zipped between them, crackling and sparking.

Holly's fork lingered close to her lips. She didn't stop watching Farid as she ate. How perfect was this? If he wanted to stick around for dessert, he was more than welcome. She pushed her plate aside and steepled her fingers, leaning towards him. 'So—'

A ringing interrupted her and she glanced at her phone.

'Oh no.' With a sigh, she lifted it. 'Work. I should take it.' Great. Just what she needed.

It sounded the death knell for their evening.

The following morning, she slammed her phone onto the worktop like she'd never been off it. Sleep had happened, but not long enough or sound enough. What should have been a fun evening getting to know Farid had flopped. She pinned her hair to her scalp, holding it off her forehead. No getting round the facts, she had to talk to Gavin.

'He's just a man.' She filled the kettle. A man like any other. No big deal. They were grown-ups with business to discuss. The teeny-weeny problem of what happened six Christmases ago stood in her way like Jim Carey in his Grinch get-up, holding out giant fingers ready to trap her if she tried to run by. These hang-ups were ridiculous. Meeting Farid had proved that. His resilience was incredible. How would she feel if their situations were reversed? She gave herself a shake. Get a grip.

Perhaps if she called Alice that would help. Alice detested Gavin, blaming him for not understanding Holly at all, for having his own agenda and for being more obsessed with forwarding his career and social status than paying attention to the people around him. Some of it verged on the truth. But Alice had only heard what Holly had told her – not the truth. How could she confess? It was bad enough as it was.

'Screw this.' She slammed a mug onto the worktop. 'So, I made a mistake.' A big one. A public one – all Gavin's family were witnesses. She screwed up her eyes. *No. Go away.* Mr and Mrs Sinclair with their shocked faces, hands pressed to their chests and wide-open mouths did not belong here.

She collected her breath. Right. What to do? Mr and Mrs Sinclair invading her head wasn't the worst of it. The hunk next door was where her mind wanted to wander off to. Had she made a cock-up there too?

Being inundated with work messages during a candlelit dinner wouldn't buy her any points. 'Bugger.'

He'd seemed cool, claiming a need to shower and sleep as he had an early rise. That meant they were ok, right? Or had he been trying to escape? Had she come on too strong? Of course she had. *Why do I have no bloody filter?* Subtlety had been sorely lacking in her advances. His hot body really got her going. Her eyes had spent the meal making out with him.

Right, stop. Work. Must work. She lifted the phone and flipped it in her hand. Gavin. Gavin. Gavin. What to say to him?

Knock. Knock. Knock.

Holly leapt and almost dropped the phone. 'It's worse than Piccadilly Circus around here.' Postman maybe? She dragged open the door. Better. Farid with his lumberjack shirt pulled up to his chin, his lopsided grin promising mischief and so much more.

'Well, hello, sailor.' So much for dialling down. But whenever she clapped eyes on him, flirting became mandatory.

'I have not been called that before, but, hello.'

'So, how can I help you this cold and frosty morning?'

'You are already helping me.'

She quirked an eyebrow. 'You mean this learning about Christmas thing?'

'No, just seeing your face makes me smile.'

She smirked and her insides cheered. Yay! She hadn't scared him off. She'd have their lonely hearts snuggled up in a rug together in no time. 'Well, much as I'd love to stand here and smile for you, I unfortunately have work to do.' She pulled down her lips but he continued to grin. Oh so appealing.

'Sorry, I left so early yesterday.' He rearranged his features until he looked almost serious. 'But as we are now on Friday and your weekend is coming up and this is traditionally our holy day, we could celebrate.'

'Are you religious?'

'For myself, not really. I'm human and I see many things that I doubt in all religions, but my family very much so, especially my parents. I respect their faith.'

'Same with me.' Holly leaned on the doorframe. 'My parents are church obsessed Christians.' The Sinclairs had been even worse. Something that made Alice badmouth them even more. They owned a whisky business for god's sake; how did that tally with religion? 'It's more churchianity than Christianity these days. None of it's for me. But I digress. What are you suggesting for Friday night?'

'Tonight, you come to my house for dinner. I cook, you sit, or drink, or both. And then we have more lessons. You tell me about Christmas, I teach you about home.'

She poked her tongue into her mouth. Do. Not. Laugh. He was cute. If he'd said, come round and we'll spend the rest of the night getting it on, she'd have made a beeline for his door. But his diversions were sweet.

'Sure. Sounds gorgeous.' She looked him up and down. 'All of it.'

'Good. I am back at five. Give me some time to warm up the house and shower, then you come when you like.'

'Sounds divine.' She clicked him a wink and he mirrored her before heading for the pickup and zooming off.

Closing the door with a thud, she returned to her desk and picked up her phone. The promise of seeing Farid later flooded her with adrenaline and energy. A pleasant sensation warmed her to the core. She wouldn't be alone and, while solitude didn't usually bother her, she relished the idea of Farid's company. Besides being the hottest thing on legs this side of the universe, he was also fun and easy to talk to.

Gavin was still on her messenger contact list. She could do this. Hitting call, she waited. It rang and rang to the point where she was ready to end it. Then it connected.

'Hello.' Such a familiar voice. Low and mild, pleasant even. They'd been together five years; it hadn't been all bad. Just the end. Caused by her poor judgement. Not his, as Alice thought.

'Hi, Gavin. It's Holly.' She tucked her hair behind her ear. Duh! What a stupid thing to say. Clearly, he could see her name and her picture. She gritted her teeth in the mirror over the bedecked fireplace.

'Yes, I know. What do you want?'

Blunt but probably best.

'To talk about the Mardicon and Co. deal.'

'Oh, right. So, why are you calling on messenger?'

'Does it matter?'

'I don't like to talk business on private messenger.'

She screwed up her face. Did he think she'd call about something personal? As if. She'd blown her chance there and wasn't going to reopen that box. 'Ok, well, give me your business number and I'll drive somewhere I get better reception and call you back. Or I'll set up a team call on the computer or whatever. I honestly didn't think it would be an issue. I just need to clarify a few things.'

'Look, never mind. No one's here, so shoot. Whatever. Go for it.'

'Right, well, I have some notes I'd like to go through with you.' She put the phone on speaker and laid them out.

'Holly, can I say something?' His voice was soft.

'Yes.' Her heart hiccupped. This was going to be personal. That tone said so.

'I just hope you're ok. What happened with us was... er, distressing, for both of us. And the way we ended. It's never sat right with me.'

'Yeah. Well, what's done is done.' Heat swelled in her cheeks. If he'd shown up with a film crew while she was naked on the toilet, it couldn't have been more embarrassing. Please, could they just forget the whole damn thing? 'Now, let's get through this.'

She steered him onto business and talked over every silence in case he tried to return to anything personal. When it was time to end the call, she barely said goodbye before hitting the red cross. She closed the folder on her notes, got up, and strolled into the living room area. It was done. She could sweep him and their history back under the carpet and look forward to her night with Farid.

She typed in several lines of code. The keyboard clicked, and her eyes roved over the screen, straying to the clock over and over. Time must have slowed down. The afternoon dragged. Finally, she gave up, shut her laptop and turned her attention to what to wear.

Jammies again? They'd definitely had an impact. Too sloppy? Was a dress too formal? She settled on leggings and a loose sweater. Revolving slowly in the mirror, she smirked at her reflection. Kind of a *Dirty Dancing* look. She'd do any kind of dancing with Farid, the dirtier the better. Flicking out her long hair, she rolled her shoulders. Not bad.

Farid's pickup rumbled up just before five and Holly sat on the sofa, tapping her foot for a highly unrespectable fifteen minutes before going round. So what if he hadn't had time to shower or do anything? Holding off wasn't an option anymore. She knocked on the door, stamping her feet as a chill wind blasted her. Shivering, she rubbed her arms. Come on. Was he in the shower? Had he heard? She knocked again. This time he came shuffling behind the door and it opened.

Oh my god. She zeroed in on pecs to die for and shimmering brown skin covered in a light smattering of dark hair, tapering to a thin line, ending at the white towel wrapped around his waist. She lingered on a few discoloured lines criss-crossing his broad chest. Scars? From when he was captured?

'Hey.' He cleared his throat and pushed his hand across the markings, as though wanting to hide them from her attention. 'You didn't give me much time.'

Time to scrape her jaw off the doormat. 'I am a bit desperate, aren't I?'

'Come in then.' He retreated into the tiny hallway, the mirror image of her own and identical in colour. Georgia had used her artistic talents to decorate this one in a more Middle Eastern style with a red and gold rug, intricate photo frames and a beautiful hanging lantern-style light fitting. Not a Christmas decoration in sight.

'I should put something on.' Farid raked up his wet hair and Holly sucked on her lip.

'Don't trouble yourself on my account.'

'You are very naughty, aren't you?' His seductive lips quirked up. 'Maybe this naughty list is something for you after all.'

'No *maybe* about it.'

He opened the living room door and motioned for her to go in. 'Please sit by the fire. I have something special for you.'

'Now you're talking.' She parked herself on the deep burgundy sofa by the fire and leaned on a cream and gold scatter cushion. Somewhere close by, Farid was moving about. When the door opened, Holly covered her face and groaned. Elf pyjamas! 'No, Farid, just no.'

'Ah, come on, why not?'

'A hundred reasons.'

He dotted into the kitchen area and returned seconds later with a large bowl and a roll of foil.

'What's this for?' Holly eyed the bowl.

'I hear roasting chestnuts on the fire is the thing to do.'

'You are ridiculous.' She fluffed her fingers through her hair, pulling it to one side.

'Am I?' He sat next to her. His leg touched hers; the heat was incredible. She sidled closer so their arms touched. A warm amber fragrance spread from his skin, drifted inside her and tickled her deep. He pulled off some foil and moulded it into a container. 'You can explain why this is Christmassy.'

'It's a song and that's all I know.'

'Then let me tell you something about home.' He placed some chestnuts from the bowl into his foil container and knelt before the fire. Looking up, he cocked his head, inviting Holly to join him. She followed, crouching on her knees, bottom on her heels. Farid took the fire irons and manoeuvred the foil into the fire. 'Home is where people eat and make food. We do this together, we talk, we laugh, we share.'

'Ok, is that my first lesson?'

'Just the beginning, Holly.' He glanced at her and she stared back. Kissing him would be glorious. *Resist. Don't screw this up.*

This ritual was obviously important to him. *Stay cool and play along.* Were rules more rigid in Syria? Maybe he wasn't used to women moving so fast. Christ, she wasn't normally like this. The need he exposed in her was raw and demanding. But there was more. Something almost spiritual.

'I don't think I even like chestnuts. I had one years ago at my grandma's and I remember spitting it out when no one was looking.'

Farid ran his forefinger over the back of her hand, tracing his fingertip from her wrist to her nail. She melted and took a shuddering breath. 'It's not about liking or disliking. It's about doing this together.' He smiled and she melted a bit more. Soon she'd be a slippery pool. 'And if you really don't like them, I have marshmallows for after.'

She laughed and leaned in, resting her head on his shoulders. A sigh escaped her. Farid put his arm around her and they fell into an easy sitting position. 'Farid.' She moved her forehead, so it touched his neck. 'Those scars on your chest. How...?'

'It's not a nice story.'

'I'm quite sure it isn't. You can tell me if you want to talk about it, but I completely understand if you don't.'

He let out a slow breath, his body rising and falling. 'I want to tell you.' His grip tightened a little. 'I'm from a good family. My father has much influence because he worked a long time in the oil industry. I had a good job.' His voice was low and melodic, almost like he was singing.

'Doing what?'

'Programming computers.'

Holly tilted her head up. 'Seriously?'

'Yes.'

'The same as me.'

'Is that what you do?'

'I work in software design, and my degree's in programming.'

'Wow. That's so strange.'

'Life's full of coincidences. But go on with your story.'

'Well, like many of my friends, we disagreed with what was happening in the country. I used my computer knowledge against the government but I got caught. Many of us were. We were held and tortured.'

'Oh, Farid.' Her chest caved like a weight had hit it. An overwhelming urge to hold him and protect him rose in her. Like a human shield, she'd repel his enemies. No one would ever hurt him again. 'What did they do to you?'

'They beat us. I had ribs broken and my arm. Then there was bombing and, in the chaos, I escape. I couldn't go home, not to live. Only to get money, a phone, basic supplies. Then I run. I was with others doing the same. We hitched rides and hid in trucks. It was crazy. When we got to the port, the boats were overflowing and dangerous. They were charging terrible amounts for passage. I paid it and left.'

'Farid, this is terrifying.'

'Yes. I had one month in Turkey, then crossed Europe through many countries. I at last get in touch with my father and he tells me he has connections in the UK and I should make for there. After four months, I arrive in the UK, then for a year, I live in a hostel as an asylum seeker. This house is a palace when I think how I lived then. Many are not so lucky. Because I had been tortured, I was granted refugee status and allowed to stay but because I was no longer an asylum seeker, I had to leave the hostel. There was nowhere to go. I lived rough for weeks and could not get work. Thanks to my father, I finally got in touch with Archie and he agreed to this arrangement.'

'Sheesh.' Holly sighed. Thank god her father wasn't here to hear this. He'd worked in the defence industry for years and was deep in the pockets of politicians, some with bees in their bonnets about asylum seekers, misterming them 'illegal immigrants' and determinately refusing to acknowledge the difference. 'That was lucky your father knew him.'

'Very lucky.'

'I can't imagine how it must feel.'

'Sometimes, when I'm alone, it's agony. I spent nights on the street, wishing I could just die.'

'No.' She bit her lip, stoppering a lump rising from her throat and shifting closer to him.

'*Ay, na'am.* But I didn't go all that way to give up. What hurts is I might never see my family again.' He bumped his ribs with a fist.

'And are they safe? Or will the government go after them?' she asked, blinking to clear her vision as tears welled.

'They're in a safe house in Turkey and I think they will stay.'

'You've been through so much.' She rubbed her hand down his thigh in a soothing motion.

'*Ya'ni*. But, look, we have chestnuts. So, don't worry.' He released her and leaned forward for the fire irons. Carefully, he lifted out the foil container. 'We should let them cool. Why don't you cheer us up and tell me something Christmassy while we wait?'

'Seriously, do you still want to learn about Christmas after what you just told me? It's so pointless.'

'Come on, tell me another song, a tradition, anything. It will make me happy.'

'Will it? I don't get how learning the bizarre rituals of Christmas can do that.'

'Having your company makes me happy.' He decanted the chestnuts into the original bowl.

'Then you could just ask me out.' The words spilled out before she could stop them.

He froze and stared at her, suspending the foil container over the bowl. Her heart pounded faster than normal. Why the hell did she say that? Always the loose cannon, firing off left, right and centre.

Then his lip curled up. 'What's to stop you asking me? Don't you British girls like to make the first move? Isn't that the modern way?'

'Yeah.' She rubbed her forehead. Gavin's face swam in her mind. 'Not sure that's my greatest strength.'

'Ok, then.' Farid laid down the bowl of chestnuts and took both her hands. She furrowed her brow but warmth spread through her veins. 'Holly, would you like to date me?'

She swallowed. This was like a proposal. Please no. Not another one of them. Especially at Christmas. 'I would, but you know I'm only staying here a month or so. So, this is just a short-term thing.'

'I understand.'

'Good, because I want that to be crystal clear so there's no chance of you misunderstanding my intentions, ok?'

'For sure, yes. So, will you date me for one month and no longer?'

'Yes. Yes, I will.'

He raised both her hands, then pressed his lips to her fingertips. Her nails grazed his neatly trimmed facial hair. Her transformation to liquid concluded. She dropped her eyelids, letting out a deep sigh.

'I take you somewhere wonderful for our first date. Somewhere special for the beautiful Holly.' He laid another kiss on her fingers, then let go.

Holly's eyes pinged open. Did he really just say that? Do that? What kind of a romantic was he?

He cracked open a chestnut, held it up, then popped it into her mouth. 'Good?'

She savoured it in her mouth, rolling it over with her tongue. The warmth of his words infiltrated every cell in her body. 'Actually, it's not bad.'

'Then you eat and I make the main course.'

She rested her back against the sofa and popped another chestnut. So they'd reached dating. Already. Fast by anyone's standards. She gave a little shrug as she grabbed a third chestnut. When she'd arrived, she'd been ready to jump straight into bed with him and dispense with dating altogether. Now they'd strayed down a more conventional path and it felt right.

'I also have this.' Farid returned from the kitchen area carrying a bag.

'What is it?'

'A game.'

Holly raised her eyebrows. 'What kind of game? Strip poker?'

Farid pulled his lips to the side, holding back a laugh. 'Not quite.'

'Russian roulette?'

'Doesn't that need guns?'

'Yeah. Not that then. So, what is this game?' Did she really want to know?

'Tada!' Farid pulled a lurid red and green box from the bag. 'I get this from Georgia. She says it will keep me busy for a long time if I can find someone to play with.'

'Christmas Monopoly.' Holly lay back and groaned. 'Oh my god. Monopoly can go on for days. That's how you want to spend the night?'

He nodded with wide eyes. *Well, why not?* She'd been pushy and fast enough as it was. And really, if he wanted to do this, then fine. Time to show him who was the boss of the board game.

'Bring it on.'

He flashed her a smile, sending deep contentment soaring into her chest. Did it matter how they spent the evening? Farid's company was gold and she'd do anything to spend more time with him.

CHAPTER NINE

Farid

Perhaps it was a reaction to living through troubled times, but Farid didn't want to waste a second. Now he'd asked Holly on a date, he wanted it to happen and fast – but properly. Fast didn't have to mean rushed. She'd left late the night before after the alcohol-fuelled game of Monopoly got competitive. She won. Meh. Maybe she'd hoped to stay the night, but he'd let her go.

He pulled on a hoody and sighed. Should he have bitten the bullet and gone for it? Back in Daraa, he wouldn't have had the chance. His family was conservative and had a bride picked out for him – before his capture. He rubbed at his chest and stared out the window. Would his father ever truly forgive what he'd done? He'd brought shame on their family. Their relationship had been rocky at the best of times. Farid wasn't devout enough and that bothered Khalif Al-Karim. But after Farid's escape, his father was the one who suggested Archie as someone to turn to. The olive branch had been dangled before him. Farid had grabbed it with all his might. If only he could see his father now.

Let him know. Apologise. Maybe time would never be enough to atone and live up to his standards. Now the family had left Syria, Khalif understood Farid's plight and his reasons for speaking out against the government but a full reconciliation? Doubtful. Khalif may come round but in his own time. Would that day come? Ever?

And what Farid wanted to do with Holly... The way he wanted to hold her, kiss her, go even further. It went against his family's beliefs. He raked his fingers through his hair. Mustn't get ahead of himself. He had a date to organise. An afternoon tea in Tobermory perhaps? That was something the Brits talked about. And waiting until evening was too long. He peered out the window and pulled a face at the sky. Low grey clouds obscured the view of the sea.

Holly wouldn't be working today. A sharp tug like a hook behind his belly button pulled him to look her way. A solid stone wall separated them. But she was there, just there. Could he go round? Did she want that? Was he being too keen? Maybe she'd arranged to meet Georgia or do something that didn't involve him. Pah. He couldn't expect to spend every moment with her. His heart plunged and roiled. What to do to pass the time until the date?

A jog around the paths on the estate might get rid of some energy. He could learn the lie of the land. After pulling on some running gear and trainers (cast-offs Georgia had passed his way), he jogged towards the main mansion; a huge stone palace Archie and Georgia let out to rich tourists who wanted to live in a Scottish Castle for a week.

Farid skirted the side of it and headed along a rising path that clung to the edge of a blustery cliffside. He'd often spotted Archie walking this way with his dogs but from below it wasn't clear where the path went. The views were probably spectacular on sunnier days. Farid rounded a bend. Ahead on the path, hand in hand, were Georgia and Archie, laughing and swinging their arms, lost in their own world. The dogs sniffed around.

What now? Interrupt their private walk? Go back the other way? Farid stopped and sighed. How lucky to be like them. He put up a silent wish. *Please send me someone to hold.*

Georgia turned his way; she blinked, and her smile widened.

'Hi.' With her free hand, she waved. 'You're very energetic this morning.'

He jogged closer. '*Ay.* So are you.'

'But I don't fancy running it.' She glanced at Archie. 'You?'

'No thanks. Definitely not up the way.'

'It's not bad,' Farid said. 'Easier when it's cold. I used to run in the baking heat. That was hard.'

'Sounds it,' Georgia said.

He pressed his lips together for a second. They knew everything about the island. They'd know a good place for a date. But should he tell them his plans? They'd understand, wouldn't they? He raised his fist to his mouth and cleared his throat. 'Where is a good place to eat in Tobermory?'

'For lunch?' Georgia said.

'Afternoon tea. I'm taking Holly on a date.'

'Oh, wow.' She beamed from ear to ear.

'There you go.' Archie nudged her. 'Not everyone on the island needs you to set them up.'

'Shhh.' She poked him with a smirk. 'There are a few places you could try. The Western Isles Hotel is lovely for a view, or the Blue Whale Café is small and intimate.'

'They sound nice.'

'What time are you going?'

'Whenever I can get a table.'

'Well, there's carol singing tonight at six if you want to join in with that after.'

'What's that?'

'It's when Archie knocks on people's doors and gives them a rendition of "Oh Come, All Ye Faithful" so he can show off his singing voice.'

'No, it isn't.' Archie gave her half an eye roll. 'It's traditional in Britain. We've arranged for people to gather at the clock and walk along the promenade singing carols. In the past, it was a way for children to make money. They'd knock on doors, sing a song and hope to get a penny for it.'

'Or a shilling to be quiet,' Georgia said.

Farid grinned. 'You two are funny. Ok, and is this carol singing about Christmas?'

'Yes. It's usually Christmas songs.'

'Then Holly might murder me if I take her to that.'

'Hmm, I forgot about that.' Georgia wrinkled her nose. 'Maybe best stick with food then.'

'Ok, thank you.'

They said their goodbyes and Farid jogged on, stopping for a few seconds at the top of the rise to look out over the murky sea. Carol singing, *ay*? He pulled out his phone and scrolled through the music he'd downloaded over the past few days. Holly wasn't here. No chance of her kicking him over this cliff if she heard what he was listening to. He popped in his earbuds and hit play on a traditional Christmas playlist. No way would he learn all – or any – of these songs before tonight. But there was joy in singing outside. Like the *adhan* echoing around the cities back home. Carol singing would be another chance for him to embrace a Christmas tradition and after he could teach Holly more about home.

He checked his phone for reception as he rounded the coast. One bar. It might be enough to call the café and book a table. Keying in the number, he tapped his toes until it connected. Success! The date was on. He increased his pace, slapping the ground until he arrived at Holly's door. He knocked, bouncing on the soles of his feet. His smile cracked his face as she opened the door.

'Hello, hello, hello.' Holly folded her arms and leaned on the doorframe. 'What's all this then?'

'Date this afternoon. You and me. Blue Whale Café at three, then something special to follow at six.'

She raised her eyebrows. 'At six?' Her brow creased slightly. 'What exactly are we doing?'

'You'll see. And wear warm clothes.'

'Warm clothes? Seriously? Not exactly what I wanted to hear.'

'Be patient.'

'I'll do my best but it's not my number one virtue.'

As the day wore on, Farid discovered it wasn't his either. Just as well he'd booked for afternoon tea because he'd never have lasted until evening. Holly, Holly, Holly. When would they be together again? Crazy, huh? Time and its tricks. Holly would be by his side in a matter of hours. He may not see his family for years. The urgency beating in his chest made every nanosecond last an hour. Time dragged slower than ever. But in the grander scheme, it was hurtling out of control. What was he doing with her? Encouraging her flirting, going along with it? Could he deliver what she wanted? He couldn't exactly practise. One shot. Make it count. Do it right.

By quarter to two, the sun was already dipping. A knock on the door. Farid jumped and sped down the hall.

'Holly?'

Her dark lashes fluttered, her plum lips sparkled and her glossy hair cascaded over the shoulder of her black coat.

'You're very early.'

'I couldn't wait any longer.' She took his hand. 'Can we just go?'

He squeezed her fingers. 'Yes. I feel the same.' He grabbed his coat and they left.

Farid steered along the track to the gate of the Ardnish Estate and onto the main road – it wasn't much wider.

'So, what are we doing at six?' Holly asked.

'Wait and see.'

'Oh, you're such a tease.'

'But you like it.'

She chuckled. He kept his eyes on the road, letting the joyful sound tickle his insides.

'We're far too early.' He checked the time on his phone as they arrived at the café.

'Ah well, never mind. Let's see if they'll let us in anyway.' Holly pushed the door open.

A young waitress approached. 'Table for two?'

'We're booked,' Holly said. 'But we're early.'

'No problem,' the waitress said. 'We have seats over here.'

Farid hung back. His eyes travelled over Holly as she tossed off her coat, revealing a low-backed grey top in soft, shiny fabric; it tucked neatly into tight black jeans. She sat, crossing her ankles. High-heeled leather boots rode up her shins, ending just below her knees. *Close mouth and sit.* Farid gave himself an internal shove and moved forward, taking a seat opposite.

Holly ran an immaculate nail down the menu. 'They don't serve alcohol. We'll have to settle for the soft stuff. Probably best if you're driving anyway. You can have some Irn Bru.'

'I like that.' Farid rolled up his shirt sleeves.

'Yuck. Grossest drink ever. But it is made of girders apparently, so you can drink it and turn into Iron Man if you like.' She raised an eyebrow, her gaze trailing over his forearms, leaving a wash of goosebumps. With a little cough, she glanced away, then screwed up her nose at the Christmas tree in the corner. Soft music played in the background. 'Ugh. This song.'

'What is it?'

'"I'll Be Home for Christmas."'

'It sounds nice.' Farid pulled the menu closer. 'Home in a place filled with love, peace and happiness.'

'Oh, Farid.' Holly rested her hand on his. 'I keep putting my foot in it. It's just that I'm not that close to my family and the idea of spending Christmas cooped up with them sets me on edge.'

'Why? What have they done to cause this...' He put out his hand, searching for the right word.

She sighed. 'I guess I'm a disappointment to them.'

'I understand this feeling. My father thinks the same about me. But why with you? You are so successful and bright.'

The waitress interrupted with a slight cough and they ordered.

Holly waited until the waitress had moved away. 'You're sweet saying those things about me, but it's not that. It's so much more petty and stupid than that. If I tell you, you'll laugh. I'd laugh too if I didn't know it was true.'

'Tell me.'

'Well, they wanted a boy and they got me.'

'Ah, that is sad.'

'But it's worse than that. They didn't just want a boy, they thought it was some kind of destiny to have a boy and my coming along ruined that.'

'Er... ok. How?'

'I told you it was crazy. My mother has this idea of a perfect family. A girl and a boy. Apparently, it always happens in her family. It worked for her parents, her grandparents, her brother. Even my father has a sister. So, in my mother's bizarre mind, she decided because she'd already had a girl, she'd have a boy next. Obviously, she didn't.'

'But couldn't she have tried again?'

'Oh, no. My mother thinks it's criminal having more than two children. I grew up trying to be a bit boyish, hoping to please her. But that didn't work. I was just me and I didn't really fit with what she wanted.'

'*Ya'ni*, they've missed out.' He ran his finger down her forearm. 'You're intelligent and confident. You have a good job and success.' Where did that leave him? What could he offer her? Once upon a time, he'd been these things too but now he chopped trees and lived on a hand-to-mouth basis. His future wasn't guaranteed. He placed his palms flat on the table. He should stop this game. But could he?

'That's kind of you but they won't see it. I know you put a lot of stock into home but I didn't have much of a home growing up. My father worked in the defence industry and we moved about with his work. I never felt settled anywhere.'

The waitress brought their drinks and they sipped them quietly. Holly's words danced around Farid's brain. What was his next move? He'd already lost at Monopoly.

Their window seat looked out over the town and the harbour. Lights began twinkling as the sun set, reflecting on the darkening sea.

'Cute, isn't it?' Holly said.

'Very.'

'The thing we're doing at six. Is it Christmassy by any chance?' She took a large gulp of pink lemonade.

Farid smirked. 'It is.'

'Seriously?'

'But we will have fun. Much fun.'

A cake stand arrived laden with sandwiches and sweet treats. Farid grinned as the waitress explained the selection. Holly's screwed up nose told him many of these were Christmassy. Turkey and cranberry sandwiches, mini yule logs and marzipan fruits got a particularly sour reaction but tasted delicious.

The café closed at five, and they went for a stroll around the village. Holly slipped her hand into Farid's and he took it; their palms burned together as they climbed the steep brae. He gazed out over the harbour, now lit fully by street lamps and reflecting the gleaming Christmas lights in the square.

'Right, tell me now, where are we going?' Holly said. 'I hate surprises.'

'Ok. Carol singing.'

Holly ran her free hand down her forehead. 'You are kidding, right?'

'No. Tonight we carol sing. Georgia and Archie are going. They are opera singers by the sound of things.'

'I bet Georgia's the one who sings the descant bits at the top of her voice.'

'I have no clue what that is.'

'Well, you'll hear it. I wish I'd brought earplugs. And it's bloody freezing out here.'

Farid wrapped his arm around her. Her height put her in exactly the right position to do the same to him and they balanced each other. 'I'll keep you warm.' His own central heating ratcheted right up. Blood pumped fast, throbbing in his veins. Holly's hair smelt beautiful, mellowing the sting of cold air.

'You better.'

Time may have passed as they stood or it might have stopped. Either way, they didn't move. Vague memories of cold, lonely nights played in the back of his mind. When he'd been huddled in a doorway with rain driving down and warmth was a sensation he couldn't recall, he'd dreamed of moments like this. Was it too good to be true? The speed was overwhelming. His emotions had been shaken up and were jammed on fast forward. A door opened in a house behind. Some people came out chatting.

'Let's go,' he whispered. 'It starts soon.'

'I don't want to move. I like this too much.'

'I do too.' He stroked her hair. 'But we can't be here all night.'

Cold wind bit as they broke apart.

One side of the main street was lined with buildings, their colourful fronts lit up by the street lamps; the other had a railing separating them from the sea. In the middle, a harbour wall jutted out and a throng gathered around the base of a clock tower. People talked and laughed. At the edge of the crowd, Farid nudged Holly in front of him.

'What are you doing?' she muttered.

'Keeping you warm.' He wrapped his arms around her from behind and leaned his chin on her shoulder, closing his eyes as his cheek touched hers. He let out a sigh through his nose that landed on her ear. She flinched and giggled.

'That's tickly.'

He shifted, but she raised her hand and pulled him back.

'I like it though. Just stay right there.'

Cheek to cheek, he held her, swaying on the spot. What a moment of beauty. Could he cling to it forever? Ending this embrace would be painful; like cutting away part of his flesh. She was in him now, deep in his soul. This physical connection was an outward gate to so much more.

He shifted his head slightly. A man flickered into view through the sparkly Christmas lights. Per Hansen smiled back.

'Hello, Farid,' he said. 'I thought it was you. Hard to tell in the dark and with all the layers on.'

'Hi, Per.' Farid straightened up and released Holly. Displaying public affection would be heavily frowned on by his parents.

'It's good to see you here.' Per turned to a woman beside him, who smiled broadly. 'This is my wife, Fenella, and my daughter-in-law, Robyn.' A younger woman stepped into view; her ice-blonde hair shone under the street lights.

'Pleased to meet you.' Fenella put out her hand. 'Per tells me all about you.'

Farid smiled as he shook her hand. 'This is Holly, my neighbour.'

Holly gave a stiff little wave. 'And he's my date.'

'Very good.'

Farid shuffled his feet. They'd been caught in a grip of affection. His stomach squirmed.

'Carl, our son, is leading the singing,' Per continued, his smile unfaltering and his eyes kind. 'He's very talented.'

'So are you.' Fenella rubbed his arm.

'The whole family are amazing singers,' Robyn said. 'I'm not musical, so I just listen.'

'You have a lovely voice,' Fenella said. 'You just need confidence. Do you sing?' she asked Farid.

'Not really. And I don't know any of the Christmas ones; I'm just here for the fun.'

'Quite right,' Fenella said.

A microphone crackled and they looked towards the clock tower. Farid spotted Georgia. She tapped the microphone and faced the crowd. 'Hi, everyone. I hope this isn't too loud. I'd like to welcome you all here and thank you for coming. This event is purely for fun and enjoyment, and the plan is to start here with a few songs, then move along the main street. We won't knock on any doors.'

'Thank heavens for that,' Holly muttered. 'Can you imagine the poor sods if this lot turned up at their door?'

'At the end, we'll make a collection but it's purely voluntary. All the proceeds will go to the new affordable housing scheme. We're lucky to have Rebekah Ama Yeboah, the founder of the scheme here tonight, and Blair Robertson and Calum Matheson, who also work with the initiative. If they sing extra loudly, we might muster a few extra pounds to persuade them to stop.'

A murmur of laughter rippled through the crowd.

'Before we get started,' Georgia continued, 'we're going to have the official Christmas light switch on. This year we're lucky enough to have our very own island celebrity to do the honours. Please welcome former Scotland striker Troy Copeland.'

Farid joined in the clapping as a young man hopped up beside Georgia.

'Bloody football,' Holly muttered. 'It's my second favourite thing after Christmas.'

'Thanks, everyone,' Troy said. 'Now, here goes. If you'll join me in a countdown. Ten, nine...'

Grinning, Farid joined in as Holly rolled her eyes. Five, four, three, two, one, zero. Troy pressed a button, and lights burst along the front. Clapping and cheering echoed around.

'Thank you, Troy.' Georgia took the microphone. 'Now, let's get singing. I have Carl Hansen here and he's going to lead us. Hopefully everyone has word sheets and Archie will get the music playing on the block rocker. The first song is "Once in Royal David's City". Please remain quiet for the first verse. We have a local schoolgirl to sing it for us. If you could welcome Catelyn Walsh.'

Applause broke out and Fenella whistled. 'She's one of my pupils.'

The opening music started up. Holly's hand brushed against Farid's. He threaded his fingers through hers and held on. The girl sang out in a clear, haunting voice. David's City. Bethlehem. A journey of around one hundred and fifty miles from Daraa. Goosebumps prickled up Farid's arms. The voices reminded him of the *adhan* and the words of home. A lump swelled in his throat and tears welled close to the surface. *Keep it in.* He glanced at Holly and she answered the look instantly. Her eyebrows raised in the middle. Words didn't come, but maybe she guessed what was going through his mind. Her fingers squeezed his, then she let go, slipped her hands under his arms and wrapped him in a tight hug. A broken sigh escaped him and he returned her embrace, holding her fast as the verse ended and the crowd joined in. No more words made their way in but the tune formed in his mind and he gently hummed it, closing his eyes and relaxing his chin on Holly's shoulder. She rubbed his back. A blissful embrace.

When the song ended, Farid released her. 'Thank you.'

'You looked like you needed a hug.'

He took her hand and they hummed their way through the next songs before moving on.

'Is this what you imagined then?' she asked.

'I don't know. But I like being here with these people. It's like a big family.'

Holly stroked his hand between both of hers. 'I don't remember half these songs and we didn't get a sheet.'

'I like listening.'

'And I like you.' She locked gazes with him and a smile brimming with understanding passed between them.

After walking the length of the promenade, they made their way back. Georgia closed the event and the crowd dispersed, dropping money into a bucket. Per chatted to Farid for a few moments. Holly didn't speak; her smile was frozen and she flicked at something on her sleeve.

'We're going for a drink. Maybe catch you in the pub,' Per said with a wave.

Farid raised his hand. The crowd swallowed Per and his family.

Holly took his arm. 'Let's just go home.'

'Ok.'

They jumped in the car and made their way back.

'What in the name is this?' Holly pulled out her phone and scrolled through messages. 'Oh my god.'

'What is it? Something wrong?' Her tone said there was.

'My dad's had a heart attack. He's been taken to hospital.'

'Oh no.'

'Shit.' She wedged her fingers into her hair. 'I need to make some calls. My mother, my sister, maybe my aunt. They're all messaging me.'

'We'll soon be home. You can do it there.'

He pulled up outside the cottage. Holly flipped her phone in her hand, staring at it.

'Do you want me to come in?' He jumped out after her. She gave him an odd look. 'Just to be with you so you're not alone if bad news comes.'

'I can't make you do that.'

'I don't mind.'

'Then yes.' She nodded. 'Please.'

'Of course.' He moved forward and held her; she stumbled into his arms.

'There's nothing I can do from here. It's out of my control.'

Farid rubbed a gentle circle on her back. 'Yes, *jamilati*, I know exactly how that feels.'

Chapter Ten

Holly

Holly hadn't seen her father for six months. Visits were scant. Rarely pleasant. Often tense. A chill crept up her spine, filtered into her veins and seeped into her chest. *Why didn't I visit more?* What if this was the end? Sharp-toothed thoughts nibbled the raw edges of her heart. Her father was in the Borders General Hospital waiting for scans. If he died now, she wouldn't have a chance to say goodbye. Her mother was with him and her aunt, his sister, had driven miles to sit with her. Alice couldn't get there from Wolverhampton and Holly was as useful as a Christmas tree without branches.

She hugged her knees, resting her head on the back of the sofa. Her mother's panicked voice nipped on the end of the phone.

'Have you any idea how difficult it is for me to talk on this silly messenger thing? Just as well Aunt Elizabeth has the daft thing installed. It's something I could do without right now.'

Holly held the phone level with her chin and sighed.

'How can you conduct business in a place with no mobile reception? Are you sure you aren't inventing complications?'

In the kitchen area, cupboards bumped open and shut. Holly craned her neck. What was Farid doing?

'Listen, Ma, you have to wait until the scans come in.'

'What do you think I'm doing? But it's awful, sitting here, not knowing.'

'I get that.'

'Easy to shut off when you're far away.' Her voice was muffled.

Holly clenched her jaw. Not the right time to pick a fight.

Farid strolled over with two mugs and set them on top of tartan coasters on the oak table. He tugged the table closer to the sofa and flopped onto the cushion beside Holly. She leaned sideways, resting her head on him. His arm slipped around her and some of the tension ebbed with the warm touch. Leaning forward, he lifted a mug and passed it to her. She sipped the milky tea, still listening to her mother. What else could she do? Nothing. As her mother kept pointing out.

When she ended the call, she smacked both the mug and her phone on the table. 'I know I'm useless but what the hell does she want me to do about it?'

'Hey.' Farid hoisted his legs onto the sofa and wrapped Holly in a tight hug. She closed her eyes and let his warmth soothe her like a balm. 'You're not useless.' His words fell softly into her hair and she yielded further into his chest. 'Distance is a cruel thing. No one can be everywhere. One day, you may face trials and no one will be with you. Today, your mother must face this without you. It hurts her, so she hurts you with words in return.

But remember, it's not a competition. You don't be guilty for how you feel. You cannot change her. Allow yourself to feel as you need.'

Holly didn't open her eyes. His words were soft, almost like a song. 'Your English is so good. I don't know many British men who could say such beautiful words.' He smoothed his hands over her hair, turning her into warm jelly.

'I make more tea if you want it. You Brits love your tea, huh?'

'Right now, I love your hugs more.' Where was this gush coming from? He'd melted her insides. Danger lurked too. If he let go, she'd have to face grim reality.

'Then that's what you'll get, *jamilati*.' He increased his grip, drawing her closer so she was tight against his chest. His fingertips gently caressed her hair, his palm stroked her cheek and her eyelids slipped shut again.

'I don't know what that means, but it sounds nice.'

'My beautiful,' he whispered.

A moan slipped from her. She couldn't do anything for her father but wait. The warmth and comfort from Farid's stroking eased the lonely anticipation and lulled her into a daze, neither sleeping nor awake, hovering in a world of heavenly peace.

A ringing sound filtered into Holly's half-conscious daze. Where was she? Lying down. Warm. The scent of amber oil permeated her dream state. Her cheek pressed against something hot. In her dream, she'd lain on a beach in Farid's arms. Had they been dressed? The heat of his skin scorched against hers, his hands on her back, her lips on his. It was fading. The noise getting louder.

'Holly.' Farid spoke close to her ear in the darkness. She blinked her eyes open; he was holding her. Not on a beach but on the sofa, her on top, moulded into him like he was a memory foam mattress shaped exactly to fit her. Her mouth was dry as she tried to move. 'Your phone is ringing.' His right hand lifted from her back and he scrabbled around on the coffee table.

She manoeuvred into a half-sitting position and he followed, supporting her as she balanced. The ringing stopped. 'Oh no. I hope nothing's happened. Ma will be furious if she finds out I fell asleep.'

'Ring back.' Farid's voice was husky. 'It's four in the morning. I hope it's not bad news.'

Holly opened messenger and with heavy fingers hit call on her aunt's little round picture. She answered on the first ring.

'Here's your mother,' she said before Holly could speak.

Ice spread through Holly's veins. Her heart hammered and she forced herself to speak. 'Hi, Ma.'

Farid shuffled in the seat behind her and curled his arm around her trembling shoulder. The affectionate nature of his concern struck low in her tummy, radiating outwards and filling her with solace.

'Dad's fine.' Her mother's tone was clipped.

'He is?' Just like that? Farid increased the pressure on her shoulder.

'Yes. It was a false alarm.'

'But... How? I thought he had a heart attack?'

'Turns out it wasn't a heart attack.' Her mother's voice lowered with every word. 'Just severe indigestion.'

'What?'

'Now he's had the medication, the situation has... eased. We're taking him home.'

Holly let out a slow whistle. 'Ok. Thank goodness.'

'Yes. It's a relief.'

'Well, you take care, Ma. And get some sleep.'

'Hmpf,' she snorted. 'Like I'll be able to sleep a wink with your father in this state. I'll have to go into the spare room to avoid the... Well, you know.'

Holly pressed her lips together, suppressing a smile. 'Yeah. Well, take care. Night, Ma.'

'All ok?' Farid said as Holly ended the call.

'Yes. Apparently, it was indigestion.'

'Oh... Like you mean, bad gas.'

'Exactly.' Holly let out a laugh. The weight fell from her shoulders; she screwed up her face. 'Gross.' She imagined her mother and aunt in the car with the windows open, holding their noses all the way home. Groaning, she ran her fingers through her hair. 'I'm sorry, what a waste of a night.'

'Not at all.' Farid stroked his fingers down her arm. 'Spending time with you will never be a waste.'

'You say the sweetest things.'

'I mean it.'

Holly turned to him. Vaguely, she could make him out in the darkness. The chilled air nipped her skin. Hadn't the heating kicked in yet? She rubbed her arms. 'Is there any point trying to get back to sleep now?' If she could return to her dream, she would. Or better, make it real.

'No, I don't think so. You know what we could do?'

'I have one or two ideas.'

'We could make a cake.'

She lolled into him with a half-laugh. 'You're mad. What kind of cake do you plan to make at four in the morning?'

'A Christmas cake, of course.'

She buried her head in her hands. 'Oh, Farid. You have no idea the fear that puts in me.' How could she ever look at a Christmas cake again? After *that* day? The day Gavin had taken her world and shaken it upside down, knocking her onto a dark path where she didn't know who she was or what to do.

'Come on. Let's do it. I have ingredients next door. I wash, then I come back and we make the cake. After that, I make you a Syrian breakfast. You will love it, *jamilati*.'

After he'd gone, Holly stayed on the sofa, rubbing her palms down her legs. What a night. Covering her mouth with the back of her hand, she yawned, then slowly got up and padded across the soft carpet to the bathroom.

The hot water revived her chilled skin and she tipped back her neck, letting it gush over her for several minutes.

Steam billowed out of the bathroom around her as she opened the door. Clattering from the kitchen meant Farid had returned and was making himself at home.

Now, how to dress for the day… casual clothes or jammies? She settled on jeggings and a long burgundy jumper with a wide neck, almost Bardot-style.

'So beautiful,' Farid said as she entered the living room.

She tucked her long brown hair behind her ears. 'Jeez, how to make a girl blush. What are you doing?'

'I have the raisins and other things but I need sherry and this I don't have.'

Holly screwed up her face. She'd done this once, a thrill of anticipation coursing through her veins, the box containing the dried fruit steeping in the sherry hidden away from Gavin until it was complete. Then Christmas Day arrived with a surprise that backfired like a Christmas cracker laced with dynamite. A bitter end for her one and only Christmas cake. 'You can't actually make the cake today. You have to let the fruit soak.'

'Ah yes. I see. But I haven't the sherry anyway.'

'You can use tea.'

'Really?'

'So my mother told me. They had to one year because my grandma had drunk all the sherry.'

'You know everything.'

'Hardly.'

'Come. Let's do this.'

How could she resist that smile? They found scales in the cupboard and weighed out the fruit. Farid leaned over, squinting as he cut glace cherries into precise quarters.

He peered up at her and grinned over the top of the knife. 'Ah, the smells. This will be a beautiful cake.'

Holly arched an eyebrow and tossed in the mixed peel. He added the cherries and poured in the tea.

'I hope this works.' She rubbed her sticky palms together.

'Have faith.' He pressed a lid onto the box, blocking the tangy citrus scent and the floral aroma of the tea. 'Now, you take a rest and let me make you a breakfast you won't forget.' Rolling up the sleeves of his blue checked shirt, he exposed his beautiful forearms; a smattering of dark hair covered them. He lifted a large shopping bag onto the worktop.

'What have you got in there?'

'Ah, *jamilati,* I have what I get in the island shops. It's not right, but it will do for now. I have eggs, fava beans, hummus, yoghurt.' He placed them on the worktop, as he named them. 'We have to use Greek yoghurt, not as good as labneh but...' He held out his palms and side pouted. 'We make do, huh? Also, I have olives, cucumber, tomatoes, pitta, haloumi and some other cheeses. They will be ok if not perfect.'

'For breakfast?'

'Of course.' He looked up and smiled. She held his gaze. Those gorgeous eyes called to her; his pupils were wide and filled with stars, reflected from the lights. 'Once you have a breakfast like this, you will never want your porridge again.'

'If you say so.'

'I do, *jamilati*, wait, you see.'

Holly sat on the opposite side of the breakfast bar, watching him. He grinned as he opened packets and took out bowls, arranging the food and mixing the herbs and spices. He set eggs to boil, sliced the haloumi and laid it on the grill.

'You don't need bacon when you have this.'

'Do you eat bacon?'

'Nope. Never tried. We don't eat any kind of pork. When this cooks, it smells like bacon. I smell it at the grill in my old lodge house, and when you taste it, you will like it even more.'

Holly smiled. She couldn't help it. Everything he did made her smile. His enthusiasm and zest. He'd had months of hardship, yet here he was cooking and laughing like someone at ease with the world. She'd had a few hours of stress and felt like death warmed up. Time to channel some of his energy and let go. What was the point of life if she couldn't enjoy it?

'Bring it on then.'

The grilling haloumi filled the room with the aroma Farid had predicted. It was only seven o'clock but the smell made Holly's tummy rumble. Some days, she couldn't face food before eleven but with a chef like this, how could she refuse? He laid it out in front of her and sat opposite. 'Ready?'

'I'm ready for anything right now.'

'Then let's do it.'

'I thought you'd never ask.' She hovered her hand over the array of dishes. 'What do I eat first?'

'You decide. There is no rules. You eat as you like.'

Holly picked something of everything, copying Farid's combinations. 'This is really good. I never thought I'd eat anything like this for breakfast.'

'It'll set you up for the day.' He licked the end of his finger and she held her breath. He glanced up and winked. 'I can tell you a story while we eat.'

'What kind of story?'

'Christmas.'

'Good god, Farid, you're obsessed.'

'This is about Christmas in Damascus. There are some Christians in Syria and in parts of Damascus, they light up the houses and put up the trees. I visit it with friends one time. And this you will like. You have Santa, the big man with a red suit, who's jolly and bright. He rides the sleigh pulled by reindeer and brings the presents to good children, yes?'

'Yes.' She arched an eyebrow. Where was this going?

'And that is the naughty list you speak of the other day.'

'Yup. I'm definitely on that.'

He grinned. 'In Syria, there is no Santa but Christian children get presents. I knew a Christian family through work and they tell me the story about the littlest camel.'

'The what?'

'No reindeer, a camel.'

Holly dipped her pitta in the hummus and shook her head. 'Is this for real?'

'Yes. The story says when the three magi visit the baby Christ, they come on camels. Now, the littlest camel is special. His journey to Bethlehem is very hard and the baby Christ gives this camel a reward. I check a word... wait one second.' He pulled out his phone and searched. 'Ah... immortality. This is the gift from the baby Christ. And every year the little camel visits the houses and puts presents into the shoes of the children.'

'An immortal camel?'

'Yes. Does that sound stranger to you than flying reindeer?'

She laughed. 'It sounds mad to me. But that's what I keep telling you; nobody knows what Christmas is about anymore.'

'Maybe these things are like the decorations on the tree. The extra bits people add on; every year it grows as people add more and more. Some old decorations... *ya'ni*... they fade and are forgotten, but the heart of the tree is the same. That's what we must find. The heart of Christmas. Not what each little extra bit means. Because different people attach different meaning to them. You might love the decoration that's like a snowflake; I might like the red flower more. We must dig deep, find the heart and what the heart means to you.'

'You should be a poet. You say such beautiful things and in a second language. It amazes me. But you've picked the wrong girl. The heart of Christmas doesn't exist for me anymore. It died and there's not a defibrillator on earth that can resurrect it.'

He slid his hand over hers and her breath caught. Such warm palms. 'Don't say that, *jamilati*. We can find it together.'

CHAPTER ELEVEN

Farid

Farid held his hand on Holly's, drowning in her twinkling eyes. All night he'd held her, restraining every urge in his body. His insides ached to kiss her and pour everything into that moment. He surfaced with a ragged gasp. How to classify or make sense of the raw emotion burning like acid in his gut? Should he just act... now?

'Will you walk with me?' he said. 'To the beach.'

Holly raised her hand to her mouth, flapped away a yawn and nodded. 'I might need a nap.'

'Sure. Let's clear up and chill first.'

'I guess a walk later will blow away the cobwebs.'

'Is that a Christmas spider story?'

Her lips curled into an irresistible smile. 'No, just a silly phrase.'

They tidied and washed up together, then flopped onto the sofa. Farid leaned back his head and closed his eyes. Three seconds hadn't passed when Holly rested on his shoulder. He leaned the side of his face flat against her soft hair. His pulse drummed an even beat in his eardrum, a little faster than usual, but steady enough to make him drowsy. He'd learned to sleep anywhere and anytime. Months in less comfortable places than this had taught him. This was a heavenly gift; the joy of sleeping beside a beautiful woman.

A fluttering movement close to his cheek stirred him. Farid opened his eyes, twitching his eyelids to adjust to the light.

'Ow. I've cricked my neck.' Holly straightened up, rolling her shoulder. 'What time is it?'

Farid checked his phone. 'Half ten.'

'Well, we've caught up a bit.' She clapped his knee. 'Shall we go for that walk?'

'*Ay, na'am.* Let's do it,' he said, though part of him would like to stay right here. He pulled on his coat and wrapped his scarf tight around his neck, up to his chin. 'The beach is always so windy.' Chill air nipped his cheeks. Holly closed the door and he clapped and stamped. His circulation had ground to a halt. Holly slipped her gloved hand into his. He glanced at it then at her face.

'We're dating, remember? Holding hands is acceptable.'

'It is for you anyway. Not so much where I come from. I'm sorry if I am slow. I don't know the rules and I don't want to be too strong or too... *ya'ni...* pushy.'

She squeezed his fingers. 'Rules are made to be broken, Farid. We don't have to play by anyone's rules. We can make up our own, ones that are right for us.'

'Ok, let's do that. You make the rules, I'll play the game.'

'Sounds good to me.' She waggled her eyebrows. 'Remember what happened the last time we played a game?'

'How could I forget?' A thrill of nervous excitement coursed through his veins, slapping him with adrenaline. He opened the gate with his free hand and stumbled through it. What game did she have in mind this time?

'Hang on, let me close it. In case some alien invaders decide to nuke the garden while we're out,' she said.

'And you think they'll use the gate?'

'If they have any manners.'

Farid chuckled. 'You make me laugh, *jamilati.*'

Hand in hand, they descended the steep slope towards the shore. Twenty-four hours ago, Farid had seen Archie and Georgia doing this. His wish had come true. He'd found someone to hold. His future was uncertain. If he could steal some joy from these moments, he was ready to assume the role of world-class thief.

They slid down the icy embankment at the bottom of the path and onto the sand. Holly ran into Farid and threw her arms around him. His chest swelled with warmth and contentment. He held her, swaying her from side to side. *I'm so glad I found you.* His hands clamped to her back but he wanted to let them roam and make discoveries. She was new and shiny, and right now, all his.

'Thank you,' she said.

'For what?'

'For being with me last night. For putting up with some strange woman and accepting me for the weirdo I am.'

'You're not weird, *jamilati*. You're you and I like you as you are.'

'Oh, Jesus, Farid, everything you say is so beautiful. Every bloody time.'

'I'm happy you think so.' He held her close, pressing his cheek to hers, imbibing her spirit and vitality, drowning in a sea of desire. 'Should we test the sea?'

Holly pulled back and gaped. 'Do you mean swim? There's no way on this planet I'd go in there in this weather, even if those aliens invade. I'd rather go with them.'

'Come on, where's that – what do you call it? – the get up and go.'

'It's got up and gone.'

He laughed and held both her hands. 'Just feet. We bathe the feet.'

'Paddle, you mean?'

'I might.' He winked. The nuances of the English language were strange. Learning them would take time and maybe it was time he had. Years ago, he'd learned the language of computers and could work magic with them. But if his words could touch the soul of a real living being, then so much the better. Archie had given him books. Some of them were so difficult but the challenge made up for the day job. Dissing the forestry work wasn't his intent but it didn't stimulate his brain enough or in the right way.

Letting go of Holly's hands, he dropped to the ground and untied his shoes. His socks came off next and his feet sank into the ice-cold sand. 'Oof.' His toes spasmed. 'This is so cold and I haven't got near the water.'

'I don't know if you're brave or crazy.'

He rolled up his jeans. 'Maybe both. But, *ya'ni*, after this year, it can't be worse.' The sand tingled in his toes, he flexed his feet and jumped up. Throwing his arms wide, he looked heavenward and inhaled the fresh air. 'All I need now is snow. Come on, let me have it. Throw down your snow, do your worst.'

'Better watch a seagull doesn't answer you.'

He smirked and strode towards the sea, still holding out his arms. 'Let it snow, bring me this winter wonderland that the songs promise.'

The edge of the sea lapped on his toes, biting like a shard of ice.

'Snow is totally overrated. It's an absolute pain in the neck and causes havoc on the roads. It's hideous to clear and a nightmare to walk in.'

'Holly.' Farid waggled his finger. 'You're spoiling the image.'

'Just telling it like it is.' She folded her arms, wearing her staunch *I hate Christmas* face. A wicked idea seized Farid and he ran towards her. She stepped back, her eyes widening.

'I won't let you spoil it. You'll be on the naughty list again.' He ducked down, pushed his head under her arm and hoisted her into a fireman's lift.

She screamed. 'What are you doing? Put me down.'

He ran into the sea. The water stung his feet and he slowed, wading in ankle deep, laughing. 'Put you down, huh?'

'No, don't you dare put me down. Get me out of here.'

'You better be good or I'll drop you.'

'Don't you bloody dare, just don't.'

He hunched over and lowered her down. She wasn't heavy but she was tall. Before her feet got too close to the water, she wrapped her long legs around his waist, her arms around his neck, and clung to him. He held her, suddenly aware of himself, of her, of how close they were. Every sensitive part of him was touching her. Her eyes found his and her lip curled slowly up. Her tense body relaxed in his arms and her face inched closer. His gaze fixed on her; he couldn't move a muscle.

Then she tilted her head, leaned forward and tugged his neck. His lips were drawn to hers and they snapped together. Fire roared through his veins. The touch shocked him and he pulled back, but Holly had him rooted and pinned. She let out a moan as she gently sucked on his lip, begging for a response. He rose to the bait, parted his lips and surrendered to the most natural action in the world. Sparks stung as Holly shuffled in his arms, drawing herself so close even an atom couldn't slip between them. She moaned again and he mimicked her without meaning to, but the sensory overload was stoking an inferno within. He focused on the touch of her lips, so soft, yet so sure. She knew what she wanted and she was taking it. His tongue brushed against hers. A jolt of electricity struck deep. He almost let go, but a secondary surge pushed his muscles tight, keeping her close. Closer. He shut his eyes, languishing in the kiss. His first. So beautiful. So precious.

Holly pulled back softly. She gasped for air but Farid kept his eyes closed, resting his forehead on hers. Awareness kicked in. His arms ached from holding her; his feet were numb in the lapping water.

'Oh god,' Holly said.

He opened his eyes and swallowed. Taking a few steps, he claimed the sand and let Holly down. She considered him, sucking in her lips.

'I'm sorry.' She met his gaze briefly, then looked away.

'Why?' He flexed his fingers. 'Not good for you?'

'Are you kidding? I was all in. But... well, I shouldn't have jumped you like that.'

He ran his hand up the back of his neck. *Keep cool.* His heart pounded overtime. 'Do I look upset?'

'No. And you did pick me up and almost hurl me in the sea.'

'I did. And that was very naughty of me. We are both now on the naughty list.' He moved forward, so they were close again, then took her face in his hands. '*Jamilati*, you are too beautiful.' Leaning in, he kissed her again. This time his hands were free. He pushed his fingers into her hair, cradling her head as they kissed long and deep.

They broke apart. Holly smiled at him. 'Maybe we should head back. There's no guarantee I'll behave myself and I don't fancy being done for exposure out here. Also, I might die of hypothermia.'

'Why? Are you planning on swimming after all?'

'Swimming? No bloody way. I'm planning on drowning in your kisses for the rest of the day.'

Farid smirked and threw his arm around her shoulder. 'Let's go back then and warm up. I now understand the need for hot chocolate at this time of year.'

'And do you think you'll prefer that to kissing me some more?'

'Ah, *jamilati*, there's room in my heart for both.'

CHAPTER TWELVE

Holly wrapped her arm around Farid's back as they ambled along the beach, his hand firmly planted on her shoulder. Being tall had always given her a sense of control. She owned her relationships, tugged the bulls by their horns and steered them as she wanted. She'd done it with Gavin right until the last stage, when everything went wrong and they'd fallen off the edge of the precipice. But something about Farid's grip gave her a sense of being led and supported. The pressure of taking charge and making decisions was removed; she relaxed, letting go of everything but this moment.

He'd said she could make the rules and he'd play along. But did they need rules? Snatching this time together filled a gap in her soul. Couldn't they let it grow organically, not push it in one direction or another?

A smile played on her lips alongside the memory of him hoisting her into the sea. The banner-waving feminist in her wanted to admonish him for daring. The businesswoman applauded him for standing up to her. The hidden princess rather enjoyed the experience.

They reached the edge of the beach where the sand met the embankment. Farid's shoes and socks nestled together among the dried seaweed, shells and marram grass. He slipped away and picked them up. Behind them was a flat area of short stubby grass and Farid plonked onto it, brushing the sand from his shapely feet. Holly watched, absently trailing her finger down her neck. His soles were lighter than the tops, which were beautifully bronzed.

'They haven't dropped off,' he said.

'What?' Holly flicked her eyes to his face.

'My toes.' He pulled on his sock. 'Ah, so warm.'

Holly shuffled in beside him as he slipped on his second sock. 'So, you not only survived crossing the Mediterranean in dangerous conditions, you also braved the Atlantic ocean in sub-zero temperatures.'

'Quite the daredevil, aren't I?' He leaned over, slipped his hand behind her neck and pulled her closer.

'You really are.'

The breeze ruffled the grass and Holly closed her eyes. Farid placed the softest kiss on her sensitive lips. She opened them again, holding his gaze. The sea and sand reflected in his sapphire-blue irises. Their lips were almost touching, separated only by a hair's breadth. 'I feel so much for you, *jamilati*.' Farid smiled, running a thumb down her cheek. Holly's insides melted;

her brain was mush. When he kissed her again, it was hot and needy. She knitted her fingers into his curls and tugged him down. Lying back on the grass, she moaned as he rolled gently alongside, supporting her head, and shifting his weight until he was partially on top of her.

They had on enough layers to keep Victorian mothers happy as they embraced. She was on the beach from her dream, basking in the heat, though it wasn't coming from the sun. It was all Farid and the scorching desire inside herself. Their kissing continued. Fast and deep. Holly thrust a hand inside his jacket, anchoring the fingers of the other in the back pocket of his jeans and clenching his tight buttock.

'Oh, *wallāh*,' he groaned. 'Are we crazy?'

'Right now, I'm completely crazy about you.' Holly tugged him back to her and resumed kissing him. Finesse be damned. This was pure, raw lust and she was surfing a wave of ecstasy, their kisses a desperate dance of lips and tongues. Lights burst in her brain. She couldn't get air to her lungs fast enough.

Her head lolled back and she gasped. Muscles all over her body were acting of their own accord: twinges of deep satisfaction, numb legs, curled toes. Only her arms felt under control. She clung to Farid, preventing him from moving. He was still except for the slow rise and fall of his back, his head buried in her neck and his warm breaths touching her sensitive skin, making her twitch and tingle. His warm weight like a blanket of calm, protecting her after a storm.

'Dear, dear,' a voice said.

Farid leapt off Holly. She pulled herself up, eyes widening. Shit. A woman with a dog wandered down the beach, tutting and shaking her head.

Farid dropped his face into his hands.

'Oops.' Holly turned to him. 'Are you ok?'

'Yeah. I just hope she doesn't know who we are.'

'I doubt she will.' She prised his hands away from his face. 'Hey. Come on. Smile.'

He leaned in and pressed a gentle kiss on her cheek. Her heart sang again. 'Ok. For you, *jamilati*, I do anything. You make me happy.' He stroked her hair and sighed. 'But we are very naughty.'

She chuckled. 'Like I said, Santa won't be visiting me this year.'

'Maybe not.' Farid smiled.

Holly trailed her fingertip down his cheek. Her senses were recovering from a flood of happy hormones and some unknown person on the beach wasn't going to spoil that. Why couldn't she release more spontaneous joy into her life? She glanced up at the sky. Clouds sailed over the sheet of blue and she huddled closer to Farid. Beauty was everywhere. So often she'd blinkered herself. Why did she refuse to see it?

'Shall we go home?' Farid said.

Home? The word threw her for a moment. Farid considered this home. Could she? What would it be like to be home? Really home. Her gaze landed on him and she furrowed her brow slightly.

'I need hot chocolate now,' he said.

'Ok.' Holly sat up. 'I could count this as an early Christmas present.'

'Really?'

'Absolutely. Why wouldn't I? Didn't you enjoy it?'

'I did.' He stared at the grass, his cheeks glowing pink through his gorgeous tan. 'I'm not sure it was the best though. And for someone to see.'

She slipped her hand over his. 'Don't sweat it. When we get back, we can refine our techniques.'

His shoulders flinched and he jumped to his feet. 'Ok. Let's go.'

Holly hauled herself up and straightened herself out. Farid had already started striding up the hill. She caught up with him and took his hand. 'Have I overstepped again?'

'No.' He swallowed and looked away. 'I feel... guilty. You get what I mean.'

Maybe he was right. Getting caught like that was pretty high on the list of embarrassing things that could happen during a kiss. She screwed up her face. But what a kiss. Satisfying and full of promise, begging to be carried on in more private surroundings. 'I am sorry. I didn't think. I acted on lust.'

'I don't blame you. I was as bad. It's just...' He ran his fingers through his hair. 'I'm not used to this kind of thing. I was supposed to have a marriage. My family arranged it.'

'What happened?'

'I was captured before we were married. It would be dishonourable for us to marry now.'

'And were you and her... you know, in love?'

'I didn't really know her. We had respect for each other, but I was resentful. I wanted to choose for myself. My father...' Farid sighed. 'My father will never forgive my sins. And this. If he knew.' He covered his face.

'There's no way he ever will.'

'But I still feel it.' He put his fist to his chest. 'Like I've done wrong and no good will come of it.'

Holly kept in step with him, not sure how to reply. The wind had blown away the moment of joy, bringing a cloud to hang over her. Why hadn't she controlled herself? She was responsible for this change in Farid. If she could have waited until she was sure they were alone. Though the spontaneity would have been lost.

'We're both adults,' she said at last. 'It's not a crime to enjoy each other's company. And we were just kissing on a beach. We weren't naked or anything.'

He cocked his head and raised an eyebrow. 'Kissing, huh? That was some kiss.'

'I'm glad we agree on that.'

With a quirk of his lips, Farid's smile returned. 'Let's keep the next one for when we're alone. And indoors. That is more sensible.'

'We lost control.'

He stopped and looked her in the eye. 'Fate brought me here. To you.' He leaned in and kissed her cheek. 'But I need it to be right.'

He started walking again. Holly's pulse rocketed and she purposefully sucked in long, slow breaths of the cold air. He didn't mean that she was 'the one', did he? All that stuff was bollocks; she believed in it as much as she believed in Santa. Relationships didn't last – not for her – they were fleeting, passing things to be enjoyed before moving on. With Gavin, she'd dreamed so hard of the perfect life, she'd forced his hand and proposed in front of his whole family, on Christmas Day, certain he wouldn't refuse, sure her future was safe with him. How wrong had she been?

This fling with Farid was only for Christmas. Come January, her bags would be packed and she'd be off. She tightened her grip on his hand. It felt too soon to leave him. She'd met him just over a week ago but she'd spent every second of every day since thinking about him. When she pared away the festive glitter, all she really fancied for Christmas was him.

He was special, but she couldn't let that change her. No man would ever do that to her.

Chapter Thirteen

Farid

After the encounter on the beach, Farid wanted to scrub himself from head to foot. He'd dreamed of Holly for days, imagining their first encounter as something immaculate, then blown it completely and been caught by a stranger having a grope on a beach.

'Argghhh.' He unleashed a silent yell at his reflection in the bathroom mirror. What an embarrassment. Could he make this right? Make it special? For whom? Her or him? She seemed to have enjoyed it. But for her, he was just another partner. A date for the short term. He'd loved every second... Until getting caught. That sullied it and made it feel unclean.

Holly was fixing hot chocolates next door and waiting for him. The idea of cuddling close to her as they sipped together warmed him deep within. But would it be the same? Had he ruined the magic with a moment of madness? Or should he shrug it off and move on?

The rain had unleashed a Mull torrent on the way back from the beach – so much for the snow he'd hoped for. Dressed in jogging bottoms and a casual long-sleeved top, he chucked his soaked jeans into the washing machine. With a deep breath, he headed round to Holly's side of the cottage. His hand hovered at the door. Knock or walk in? A compromise – he knocked, then opened the door. 'Can I come in?'

'Of course. Are you dry now?'

'Yes. All good.' He strolled into the living area, frisking up his damp hair.

Holly raised her chin and her nose twitched. 'You always smell divine.' Picking up two glass coffee mugs, she ported them to the coffee table. The warm chocolate aroma floated through the room with her.

'Thanks.' He flopped down and adjusted the reindeer cushion at his back.

'This is one of Georgia's bizarre flavours of instant chocolate from that selection she left me. I don't have cream, marshmallows, whisky or whatever else people put in them to fancy them up, but I did find these cool glasses in the cupboard.'

'It looks gorgeous, like you.'

'Seriously.' She slapped his knee as she sat. 'You're such a charmer.'

He cradled his glass, heat oozing into his veins. His jumbled brain wanted to think and breathe. But if he left Holly now, all he'd want would be to come back to her. Should he confess his inexperience? Would that scare her away completely? He'd stolen his first kiss but now he was in some weird kind of limbo.

'Farid.' She raised her hand to his face and stroked his cheek. 'Are we still ok?'

'Yes. I'm always ok with you. I'm just not sure what to make of what happened.'

She rested her head on his shoulder. 'Chalk it up as an experience, I guess.' A knock on the front door made her sit up. 'Is that my door or yours?'

'Yours. Too bad if it's mine. I'm not in.'

Holly chuckled as she got up. Farid cradled his glass, staring into the fire until the flames mesmerised him. Chatter wafted in from the hall. Farid tuned in to Georgia's voice. He downed his remaining chocolate and stood. Time to go. He couldn't stay here. Being with Holly was important. But he had to think. Getting caught by a stranger was one thing, Georgia another. She knew they were dating. Dating. Hell. What did that mean for them exactly? How would it play out? So many questions.

'*Marhaba*, Georgia.' He shuffled into his shoes in the hall. 'Holly, I'm heading back now. I must sort things for work tomorrow. I see you soon.'

'Sure.' Her brow creased in the middle.

'I'm going too,' Georgia said. 'If that's ok with you, I'll let Robyn know ASAP.'

'Yeah, it's fine,' Holly said. Farid edged past her, aware she was eyeing him directly while talking to Georgia.

He made for the gate, not looking back, and heard the door close.

Georgia caught up with him on the path. 'I'm so glad you two are getting on so well.' She patted him on the back.

'She's a beautiful neighbour.'

'Aw.' Georgia tilted her head. 'That's so sweet.'

He gave a little smile, but his eyes strayed to the window. Hopefully, Holly would understand. Putting space between them for breathing time was ok, yes? Or would she think he'd abandoned her cold? His stomach twisted.

'I know you don't celebrate Christmas, but would you like some lights or a tree? I can get you anything you like,' Georgia said.

'*Ay, na'am.* Some nice lights for out here. That would be beautiful.'

'Sure. I have loads at the house. I'll bring them up later.'

'I can pick them up tomorrow on my way to work.'

'Ok. Great.'

Hours couldn't have passed any slower. The acute torture of having Holly through the wall and out of reach pierced every atom of Farid's soul. Going around and giving in would be easy, but was it smart? What did he want to happen next? Did he want to keep seeing Holly? If he did, what were the consequences? This relationship couldn't stay chaste until their wedding night. Not at the rate they were heading. He snorted aloud. Wedding night! Holly was the modern woman personified. She lived alone, worked alone, and was self-sufficient. Weddings didn't figure in her life.

So where did that leave him? He could go back, get his clothes off and sleep with her. They could do that every day and every night until she packed her bags and left. But what then? Would he look for someone else and start again? Would it ever be the same? Were these feelings a complete lack of experience shining through? He could do it just for the sake of it. Holly could be his first – the one he could laugh about in years to come. No, that would never happen. What if he'd struck gold first time?

'Argh!' He threw his head into his hands and growled. Why so confusing?

After barely sleeping a wink that night, he got up early and left for work in the pitch black. Forestry wasn't feasible in the dark, so he parked up next to the area they were clearing and sat, tuning the radio and keeping warm. Faint music played intermittently between the fuzz. Eventually, light peeped through and Farid got out and stacked the logs before Per turned up.

'Morning.' Per rubbed his hands together; a long puff of air streamed as he spoke. 'It's bitter.'

'I'll soon know how a snowman feels.'

'You and me both, son.' Per rubbed the pink tip of his nose. 'I could give Rudolph a run for his money.'

'This is the reindeer who can fly?'

'The very same.' Per laughed. 'Sounds ridiculous when you put it like that.'

When Mike arrived, there was enough friendly chat to take Farid's mind off everything.

'We had some great news at the weekend,' Mike said. 'I'm going to be a grandad of sorts. My wife's daughter is pregnant.'

'Is that Autumn?' Per said.

'Yup. She's due at the end of April.'

'Wonderful,' Per said. 'Our eldest granddaughter, Polly, is almost three now and her little brother, Rory, is nearly one. It went fast with my own children but it's even faster with grandkids.'

Farid heaved the logs on top of each other, stacking them neatly. Hearing about these families was fine, but his chest stung. What about his family? When would he see them again? Feel Mama's hugs. Listen to his sisters giggling and grumbling. Even have Baba cross with him about something. He slammed down the last log. Who knew when? If ever.

With three weeks until Christmas, the nights came early. By half-past three, the light was fading significantly and Per called it a day.

'No point in struggling on if we can't see; we'll just make costly mistakes. Go home, guys, enjoy your evening.'

Farid hopped into the pickup. The lights. Damn. He was supposed to pick them up from Georgia that morning. Hopefully she wouldn't mind him being several hours late. He drove to Monarch's Lodge and pulled on the handbrake.

Georgia came out before he'd left the car. She waved and hurried around to his door.

'Sorry.' He clicked it open. 'I forgot this morning.'

'That's ok, I've been here today anyway. We're not opening the shop on Monday and Tuesday during the winter. Just as well really. Autumn is in the grips of morning sickness.'

'Mike said.'

'Yeah, poor girl. Her husband's got the full-time job of waiting on her hand and foot while she rests up, so it has some perks. Funny though, I was sure Robyn would get pregnant first. I had money on it, but I was wrong.'

'Is that Per's daughter?'

'Daughter-in-law. She's married to Carl.'

'I met her at the carol singing.'

'That was a good night,' Georgia said. 'I didn't get much of a chance to talk to her. I must visit her soon.'

'You like to know everything, huh?'

She pulled a face. 'Eek. I do. I'm too nosey for my own good sometimes. Anyway, here are the lights.' She handed over a box. 'They should work outside and I've checked the batteries. If you need any more, give me a shout.'

Farid put them on the passenger seat and drove back to the cottage. Utter darkness shrouded in like a thick velvet curtain over the world. He scurried inside and switched on the living room and hall lights. Cool. That lit most of the small garden. Enough to get his bearings anyway. He unpacked the fairy lights inside the doorway and checked they were working before stringing them along the little fence. A lump formed in his throat. All the people he'd spoken to today were filled with thoughts for their families and friends. People they could go and see, check if they were ok, and hug. That was luxury. Not cash or fancy things.

Some of the lights were like little lanterns interspersed with tiny silver bells that tinkled as he looped them over the posts.

Holly's door clicked open and she leaned on the frame, folding her arms, lit from behind by the warm glow in her hallway. 'What are you doing?'

'Putting up my Christmas decorations.'

'You're relentless, aren't you? Are you just trying to annoy me with more Christmas stuff?'

'No. It's like lighting candles for my family. I cannot be near them but when I see the lights, I think of them. I send pictures later and show them my Scottish garden.'

Holly jumped off the doorstep and strode down her path like she was on a mission. What was she doing? She swished open the gate and nipped to Farid's side. 'Can I help you?' She touched his arm.

'Don't you hate all this?'

'I don't like Christmas, but I like you.' She rubbed her hand up and down his jacket sleeve. 'I didn't mean to scare you off yesterday.'

'You didn't. I needed time to make sense of things. It moved so fast.'

'I know. But I missed you so badly all afternoon and today.'

'Me too, Holly.' He wrapped his arms around her and she held him in a grip lock. Raising his hands to her hair, he stroked her. She placed a delicate kiss on his cheek and the heat rushed back.

'Let me help you,' she said. 'We can put up these lights as a symbol of peace and hope.'

'Thank you.'

'The world is a cruel place.' Her words fell softly in his ear. 'You miss your family so much but you can't go to them. I could go to mine anytime but I don't want to. Maybe I should. Maybe if I was in your position, I'd miss them as much.'

'You would.' Farid caressed her back. She had on thin pyjamas and a loose cardigan; she must be freezing. 'My relationship with my parents was... tricky. But now I'm so far away, I miss them. I can't... *ya'ni,* what's the word...? Make it good.'

'They'll be proud of you now. You're a survivor. You're brave, you're strong. And maybe one day you'll get to go home.'

'No.' He shook his head. 'It's too dangerous. And my family cannot come here. They're too...' He clicked his fingers. 'They like things to stay the same.'

'Traditional?'

'Yes. And Turkey is already a big change for them. For me to go back would be crazy. This is my home now and there are many things I like. I have to keep seeing good.'

'It's so hard.'

'Yes. But not impossible. *Ya'ni...* this could be your home too, no?'

She pulled back and stared at him. 'It's just a place like any other. There's nothing to keep me here.'

'Nothing?' He quirked his eyebrow.

She looked away, her expression uncertain. Probably wise. He mustn't hang too much on what they had here. She obviously had no intention of altering their deal. One month, that was all.

'At first, I didn't think I could find home here. But now... maybe,' he said.

'Come on, let's hang the lights.' She took the end of the string, and they dotted them around the garden until it was boxed by a perimeter of twinkling stars.

'Beautiful,' Farid said. 'Now, will my phone take a good picture in the dark? Then I send it to my family.' He held it up and snapped.

'Do you want to eat with me tonight? Or is it best not to on a school night?'

'A school night?'

'It means when you have work the next day. I guess parents always tell their kids they're not allowed to do fun stuff on a school night.'

'Ah, yes. I would like that but I must first go to the village and buy food. I have nothing left. I do that now, then I shower and change. I can come around later. That ok?'

'Anything's ok with me.' She reached up and pecked him on the cheek. 'I can't imagine ever not being happy to see you.'

Chapter Fourteen

Holly

Holly leaned on the breakfast bar and tapped it with her fingernail. Her heart urged her to jump in the pickup and go with Farid, but no. He still needed space; she could tell. And she had work to do. Messages from Gavin had popped into her inbox. No matter how much she pretended they didn't exist, they wouldn't go away. Her brain was conditioned to avoid anything with his name on it. But it was four thirty and if she wanted to resolve this today, she had to bite the bullet.

'It's just work.' She poured boiling water into her mug. Strong coffee was a necessity when facing Gavin – even his words in an email.

Now she'd thrown her concentration out of the window, she could barely focus on the screen. Her brain wanted to pull up images of Farid and scroll through virtual screens filled with his gorgeous smiles and warm glances. 'Why am I so infatuated?' Tension rippled through her shoulders. She suspended her hand in front of her and it seemed to vibrate. 'It's like I've got the bloody shakes.'

She pulled up Gavin's email and curled an eyebrow as she read his business jargon. The man was a plank in a suit. What had she ever seen in him? With a dry laugh, she shook her head. He was still single too – as far as she knew. He hadn't replaced her. Would he ever? Or would he die a lonely old man? Why did she care? 'Ha!' What was she thinking? She was just as bad. There was every likelihood she'd be the same. Maybe they'd been made for each other after all. But in fifty years' time, it wasn't the dull man in a suit she saw sitting by her on the old sofa. No, no... It was Farid, of course.

'I'm off my head.' She jumped to her feet and scooted for the shower. *I should put it on cold.* It might shock her back to sense. But feelings were creeping in, swirling around like mist and invading her soul when she wasn't looking. Beyond the lust, Farid existed as someone she liked, cared for, and was invested in.

She braved the cold water for a few seconds before pushing up the temperature and sweating it out on the hottest setting. Her skin was red and sensitive when she came out. Steam filled the room. She perched on the loo seat, rubbing herself dry, not wanting to leave the heat. The house was warm enough but her room was on the chilly side when she entered it. She pulled on her leggings and a loose top. Her whole life was one long jammy-fest at the moment, but if Farid was coming for dinner, she should make herself slightly more respectable.

She lifted her laptop onto the sofa and carried on working. Some time later, Farid's door thumped shut and she guessed he was showering before he came round. Time ticked on. Maybe it had only slowed inside her brain but her concentration was wavering again. Where was he? Should she put on some food? Had he changed his mind?

A thunderous knock on her door had her almost drop her laptop. 'What the hell?'

'Holly, come quick.' Farid's voice called from the hall. 'Really quick.'

She slammed the laptop shut, leapt to her feet and ran into the hall.

'Get your coat. You need to come now.'

'What's going on?' She grabbed her coat from the hook, threw it over her shoulders and followed Farid out of the house. Instead of moving to the gate, he skirted around the side towards the back garden. Holly's eyes widened. 'Holy shit!' The sky was alight with lasers and beams of green and blue. 'Is that the aurora borealis?'

'It's a sign; a message from my family. They saw the lights.'

'Oh, Farid.' Holly slipped her arms around him.

'I know it's crazy.'

'Who cares? If it gives you hope.'

He squeezed her tight.

'I should message Georgia about this. She'll kill me if I don't. She's always wanted a photograph of the aurora. Two secs.' She nipped inside, thumbed out a quick message telling Georgia to get into the garden and look outside, then grabbed a furry blanket from the bedroom and headed back out.

Farid had taken a seat on a bench at the end of the back garden close to the edge of the headland. Holly parked herself beside him and slung the blanket over them both. His arm snaked around her shoulder and she cuddled up.

The lights blazed, reflecting in the sea like swirling ribbons of colour. Farid moved away for a few minutes, trying to capture the scene on his phone, then scooted back beside her. Slowly, the colours faded until only a hazy glow on the horizon remained.

'Holly.' Farid's voice was husky.

'Yes.'

'I'm sorry for yesterday.'

'Why?'

'Because everything moved so fast, then that lady. I did not treat you with the magic you deserve.'

Holly rubbed her temple against his shoulder. 'It seemed pretty magical to me. Annoying that we got caught in the middle of things, but so what?'

'I turn into a crazy madman around you. I can't control myself.'

'I'm not sure I want you to.' She smoothed her hand inside his open jacket and up his chest. In the hasty, desperate kiss of the day before, she'd missed the finer points of his hot bod. 'I like the idea of you losing control.'

'I really like you, *jamilati.*'

Holly continued her exploration of his chest, rolling her palm across it. 'Farid.'

He turned to face her and she moved her fingers to his cheek.

'You're so lovely. I thought it the second I saw you. If you hadn't thrown that elf suit at me, I might have grabbed you on the doorstep of Georgia's house.'

He let out a brief laugh. 'Always so naughty.'

'That's what you do to me. You make me lose my cool. You turn me to mush. I'm not sure if you came to any conclusions when you were thinking yesterday. But that's my tuppence worth.'

'What?'

'Another silly phrase. It's just my opinion. We both make each other behave like lust-filled teenagers.'

He snorted a short laugh. 'And get caught like them too.'

'That woman probably thought we were some annoying tourists and she'll have forgotten about it by now.'

'You take it much better than me.'

'Only because I know what it's like dealing with humiliation.'

'Oh, *jamilati,* I didn't mean for you to—'

She held her finger to his lips. 'I'm joking.' He took hold of her finger and pulled it away, then leaned forward and placed one of his impossibly soft kisses on her cheek, missing her mouth by millimetres. What a tease. 'Farid.' Her words fell like a whisper as she chased his mouth.

'I want us to be together but I want it to be right.'

'Not a grope in the dark on a bench in the back garden then?'

'A kiss under the stars at Christmas might work.' He wrapped his arms around her waist, drawing her closer and their lips met again; soft at first. But Holly wasn't patient. *Control.* She fought to keep that thought in her head as her hands slid up his body inside his jacket. *Take it easy.*

He pulled back and stroked her face before placing a series of gentle kisses on her cheek. 'You don't like going slow, do you?'

'Sorry, is it that obvious?'

'Yes. But I want you to have everything and not feel... used.'

'I don't feel that at all. That was the perfect Christmas kiss.'

He arched his eyebrow. 'Really?'

'Yes.' She knelt on the bench, making herself taller than him, peeled back his jacket collar and dipped her head to kiss his neck. He groaned and she smiled into the kiss. Energy surged through her and she carried on, kissing down his throat, pulling the neckline of his shirt and going for his shoulder. 'Now, please, can I open my Christmas present?'

'Do you mean me?'

'Of course I do. You really are all I want for Christmas.'

'Then, *jamilati,* I'm yours.' He smoothed her hair. 'There's no one like you.' He leaned up and kissed her, holding her face. Electric heat poured from him, leaving Holly breathless. 'I give myself to you.' He rested his forehead on her neck and hugged her.

'Let's go inside. I'll take whatever you've got and you can do what you like with me.'

His arms gripped her tight, almost crushing her. 'All I want to do with you is make you happy.'

'I'll take it. It sounds amazing.'

CHAPTER FIFTEEN

Farid

The rug was soft on Farid's back. The fire embers crackled in the grate. Holly's beautifully naked body straddled him in the red glow, her shadow dancing on the ceiling as she rocked on top of him.

She was uninhibited and free, guiding Farid's hands everywhere she wanted them and he obliged. Moaning, she arched her back, pushing her glorious breasts forward. Such beauty. He pushed himself into a sitting position, and she gasped; he wanted to look in her eyes. Pulling her close, he locked his gaze on hers and she returned it. A fierce light burned in her wide ink-black pupils. The heat of her skin against him sent rocket fuel pumping through his veins, but he held on, alternately kissing her, then pulling back and holding eye contact.

'Oh, Christ.' She braced her hands on his shoulders, rocking faster. Her eyes slipped out of focus and she breathed rapidly before her head dropped into the crook of his neck. He wanted to hold her, soothe her, kiss her some more. He tried but he couldn't hold back any longer. *Air.* He gulped for it, then the world exploded around him, shattering atoms everywhere.

Holly nuzzled his shoulder and caressed his back.

He couldn't move. Wrapped in her arms, he was safe and he clung to her, prolonging every last sensation. She moaned and jiggled a little, letting out a half-sigh, half-laugh.

'So good,' she whispered. 'So, so, good.'

'*Bahebek, jamilati,*' he said.

'What does that mean?'

I love you, my beautiful. He kept the words in his head. It was risky enough but it was exactly how he felt. Love saturated every part of him, swamping him. The urge to pour some of it into her burned him. Now they were joined by this love. 'Merry Christmas, my beautiful.' He stroked her back.

'Merry Christmas? It's still three weeks away.'

'But I am the gift that keeps on giving.'

'Ooh, Farid.'

'Is that me on the naughty list too?'

'Oh, no. You're definitely on the nice list. That was very nice and you've just offered to give it to me again. Extra nice points for that.' She climbed off him, giggling. 'You are such a beautiful man.'

He closed his eyes. She was kissing him again. There was no stopping her. He rested back on his elbow, angling his head and teasing her. Another human initiation test could be ticked off his life list. He'd survived his first time. And he hadn't failed, or she wouldn't be jumping back for more so soon. His chest swelled and the last vestiges of tension ebbed from his shoulders. Lying back, he pulled her on top of him and she squealed.

'You are too damn sexy,' she said in between kisses.

He rolled over, pinning her under him. And, *Wallāh*, she was beautiful. The power of love burning inside him was overwhelming. He wanted her all over again. 'And so are you. You make me a wild beast. I cannot control myself. I want you so bad.'

'I'm sure I want you in equal measure. So, why don't we go to bed?'

Soft blankets enveloped them as she lay on the firm mattress beneath him. He dipped in and kissed her. The stars twinkled in the pitch-black sky beyond the window as he spilled his soul into her, showering her with all the feelings in his heart while she worshipped his body. He was a god and she was his goddess. Afterwards, they twined together in the warmth, and he pulled the fur blanket over them, snuggling in and keeping her close. Sleep came quickly but it didn't last. He woke. His legs were restless.

Perhaps he should have told Holly this was his first time. But why drag it up? Would she care? Was it important? She might have guessed from his obvious lack of preparation. At least she was a modern woman who travelled with every eventuality covered. Something else nipped at his brain. He sagged into the pillow. What was it? Why couldn't he fall into a deep and beautiful sleep? But of course. This was stolen time. Holly was only here for the next few weeks. Barely a month. One month. Then what? She would disappear. How could he face the world alone now? Again. After this. He rolled in behind her and held her close, pressing his nose into her cheek.

What should he do? Revert to his original plan? Use this as experience? Thank her, kiss her goodbye, and move on? Random images of faceless women played in his mind. Would any of them touch his soul the way Holly had? Was this inexperience? All he knew was how he felt around her and what joy it brought. When they cooked and ate together, when they walked together, talked and laughed. And now this.

She shifted so her face was buried in his neck. A tune he'd heard on the radio that morning floated into his head and he hummed it. His throat vibrated on Holly's warm brow as he went through the notes.

'Farid,' Holly mumbled.

'Mmm.'

'No more Christmas songs.'

'I don't know what song it is.'

'"The First Nowell".'

He smirked. How appropriate for a night of firsts. He hummed again, the chords mellow and soft. Holly breathed on his neck but he kept going. His fingers wound their way into her hair, stroking her. As he finished the song, he whispered to her in Arabic, telling her everything he wanted, knowing she wouldn't understand a word.

Farid's eyes opened but his brain hadn't caught up. From the bed, nothing through the small square of window was visible, but it seemed to be getting brighter. Had the aurora returned? His phone was still in the living room with his clothes, exactly where they'd discarded them the night before.

'What time is it?' Holly mumbled.

'*Yina'an!*' Farid untangled himself from the blankets, and Holly, and jumped up. 'I have work. I see light. It's morning.'

Holly sat up, taking some of the blankets with her. She switched on the lamp. 'Are you sure?'

'*Ay.*' Farid bolted into the living room and spied the clock. Eight fifteen. *Nooooo.* He started work at eight thirty or soon after when the sun rose fully. He pulled on his jeans, not bothering with his shirt, boxer shorts or socks; they were about to be slung in the wash anyway. His shoes were in the hall and he scrambled through to get them, colliding with Holly in the doorway.

'Whoa.' She staggered back, securing the ties on a fluffy robe.

'Sorry, *jamilati.*' He dipped in and kissed her cheek. 'I had a beautiful time with you. You wore me out and I sleep too long. I must wash and get ready for work. I don't like to be late.'

'Will you come back later? Or have I scared you off again?'

He smiled. 'I come as soon as I can. *Bahebek, jamilati,*'

'Merry Christmas to you too.' She grinned.

I love you. He smirked as he pulled on his shoes and jacket and ran next door, ignoring the wind's sting.

The sun was up when he left the house and he raced the pickup along the track towards the forestry area. Per and Mike were already busy marking out a felling section.

'So sorry.' Farid approached, panting; his feet crunched through the undergrowth and dead wood. 'I didn't mean to be so late.'

'It's not a problem,' Per said. 'This is the Hebrides, nothing happens quickly.'

Farid smiled and rubbed his cheeks. 'I slept late. These mornings are so dark.'

'Yeah,' Mike said. 'I hate getting out of bed when it's dark and cold. It's the worst thing about winter.'

'Did you see the northern lights last night?' Farid asked.

'No,' Mike said and Per shook his head.

'I watched them with Holly from the garden. They lasted about twenty minutes, maybe more. It was awesome.'

'Amazing,' Per said. 'I've seen them a couple of times here and once in Norway. When my grandmother was alive, she lived there. They're different every time.'

'I've never seen them,' Mike said. 'You're a lucky guy.'

'Yeah, I guess.'

'Holly seems nice.' Per switched on his laser measure. 'I hadn't met her before the carol singing. Is she from the island?'

'No. She's just here for a short time.' The truth of the words stabbed Farid. Per's expression was neutral. He had a kind face that always looked happy, but was there a hint of something else? Perhaps he wondered why Farid was dating someone who wouldn't be around for long, or perhaps judged him for it. Did Per think him shallow and inconstant? 'She works from home so she can have her work anywhere. She likes to travel.' Did that make it sound even worse?

'Robyn does that,' Per said. 'She has a business she runs remotely from here. She's an island girl but used to be based in Manchester and she was away for years doing that.'

'And she came back to run her business here?'

'First, she came back to help her mother save her hotel business, then she and Carl got together and she decided to stay.'

'Very romantic.'

Per smiled. 'Maybe Holly will do the same.' He patted Farid on the shoulder.

'Let's hope, huh?' But his heart was full of doubt. Holly liked him; he was certain of that, but was it enough? She was strong, stubborn and driven. Hanging around in one place for a man wasn't her style, and was he worth it anyway? When he boiled it down, he only had his body to offer her and once she grew bored of that, there was nothing else.

Chapter Sixteen

Holly

Holly checked her make-up in the old-fashioned three-way mirror in the bedroom. The quaint little room was perfect shabby chic and so utterly Georgia. Tourists would adore the country cottage style. Holly could take it or leave it. Behind her, the bed was still a mangled mess of covers and blankets. She smirked and a tremor of glee ran through her. What a delicious night she'd had. She pouted her sparkly lips and flicked her long, straightened hair over her shoulders. 'Still got it, babe,' she told her reflection with a wink.

Farid called her *jamilati* all the time, which apparently meant 'my beautiful'. Well, she could do worse than being his beautiful. Gavin had told her she was a classic beauty back then, before the split. They'd always looked quite the pair at functions, him in his slick suits and her with killer heels, long legs and short skirts. Now, the idea of a smouldering-hot Farid on her arm in his lumberjack shirt spiked the gauge on her core temperature more than a blazer and tie.

Getting in the car was like stepping into a fridge. Holly flipped on the blasters to full pelt as she drove along the track. She had loads of projects on the go, but why turn down another one? Especially as it was on the island? Mostly, she preferred her own company when she was working but the isolation here was a whole new ball game and the opportunity to talk to someone else was appealing.

After the night she'd had, she wanted to sing. The first thing that popped into her head was "Holly Jolly Christmas". Like a brain worm, it burrowed deep in her mind and she kept repeating it. Who cared if she hated Christmas? The song summed up her mood. Maybe Farid was right; Christmas wasn't this or that but something for people to enjoy in their own way. She'd had a lifetime of shitty Christmases and a culmination event six years ago, but if she threw that thought away and embraced the fun, where was the harm? Especially if she translated embracing the fun into embracing Farid. That she could do.

She journeyed south along ridiculously narrow and twisty roads. Of all the places she'd lived, none had been quite so dramatic. She'd started off in Northumberland where her mother came from but she barely even remembered that. Some people said they still heard it in her accent but she'd been all over since then, from Helensburgh to Hullavington, from London to Edinburgh and then some. Some places she couldn't recall the names or what they looked like. Now, she was aiming for an out-of-the-way village called Carsaig, where Robyn Hansen lived. They'd met at Georgia's wedding and fleetingly again at the carol singing on Saturday. Georgia had called around on Sunday with a proposal. May as well check it out. Robyn ran a marketing company and was looking for web design for a client. Nothing was to stop Holly from doing this remotely but she wanted to get out and move. Sitting in the cottage all day was limiting and if she was only here for a short period, she should make the most of it.

The views were a refreshing change and she pulled up in Carsaig just over an hour later, energised and ready to hit the day running. Robyn opened the door of a jaw-dropping house set on its own at the end of a short lane with a large, flat surrounding garden, leading to a private beach and jetty. The front door was in an old cottage but it had been magnificently extended with a modern timber building to the side.

'Thanks for coming.' Robyn led Holly through the older part of the house, mostly taken up by a gorgeous country kitchen.

She blinked as she stepped into the open-plan living area. 'This house is stunning.'

'We built the extension,' Robyn said. 'It was just the cottage when we bought it.'

'I love it.'

'Do you mind sitting in here or would you prefer to go into the office?'

'Here's fine. Though the view's a bit distracting.' The floor-to-ceiling windows looked out over the bay.

'Isn't it?' Robyn said. 'Would you like a coffee?'

'I could murder one.'

When Robyn returned with two mugs, Holly had her tablet out ready.

'Thanks.' She sipped the coffee, then placed the mug on a side table. 'So, do you want to talk me through what you're after? And I'll see if it's something I can do.'

'Sure.' Robyn tucked her long, ice-blonde hair behind her ears and took a seat. 'Carl used to work in software development, so he's mocked up this demo for me, but it's too far out of his field for him to complete the whole project.'

'Can you email it to me and I'll study it on here?' Holly woke the tablet.

Robyn clicked away on a laptop, sending files and Holly looked through them as they chatted.

'Wow,' Holly said. 'This is big.'

'Yeah, is it too much for you to take on?'

Holly sucked in her lip as she scanned through the mock-up. 'It looks really interesting and it's definitely something I can do.' She carried on down the page. 'I want to say yes.' But another project she was working on lingered in her mind, the Mardicon and Co. job she was liaising with Gavin on. It was big as well but her heart wasn't in it. The thought of working with him turned her stomach. But this was too big to pull off alone unless she wound up the Mardicon job quickly. 'I'm not sure I can do it in the timeframe.'

'Carl might be able to help if—' Robyn pulled a pained face and put her hand low on her tummy.

'Are you ok?'

'Yeah, sorry. Just a twinge. Must've eaten something dodgy.'

'Eek, I hate that feeling.' Holly furrowed her brow. Robyn blinked and bit her lip. Something in her expression wasn't right, but she dipped her gaze to her laptop and started typing.

'Can you let me know about Carl?' Holly said. 'I have other people I could try if he's not able to.'

'Ok.' Robyn got to her feet. Was she deliberately arranging her face to appear happy? Holly was the mistress of that in the office but wasn't sure she'd recognise it in someone else. Robyn's smile didn't seem to reach her eyes, but maybe that was just her way. 'Would you like to stay for lunch or anything?'

'Thank you, but I'll get on. You don't look too good. Maybe you should lie down. Indigestion can be a right pain. My father had terrible indigestion at the weekend and was taken to hospital thinking it was a heart attack. They ran all sorts of scans and ended up giving him a bottle of Gaviscon and sending him home.'

Robyn let out a little laugh. 'Oh dear, that sounds awful but funny in its own way.'

'I can laugh now. My mother was raging and unimpressed at having to deal with the aftermath.'

'Oh dear.' Robyn walked Holly out to the car. 'Thank you for coming.'

'No problem. It was a beautiful drive. You're so lucky to have a place like this.'

'Yes, we are,' Robyn said. 'And Carl's family are like a second family to me too. You know my father-in-law, don't you? He works with your boyfriend.'

'You mean Farid?'

'The man you were with at the carol singing.'

'He's not really my boyfriend. We're just seeing each other. I'm leaving after Christmas, so it's a short-term thing.' She had to keep saying it because it reminded her of the deal.

'I see. Well, take care on the roads.'

'Thanks. Speak soon.' Holly jumped in the car and whizzed off along the bendy road, slowing straight away as a herd of cows ambled across the road. 'Well, hello, cows.' She tapped the wheel. A pang tore through her ribcage and pierced her heart. Saying aloud that Farid wasn't her boyfriend was like disowning him.

Once the cows had finished their road crossing – and they were in no rush – Holly made her way northwards again. When she reached the ferry port at Craignure, she pulled into the car park and took out her phone. Reception was patchy on the island but it worked here. She keyed out a number and waited for it to connect.

'Holly?' her father's voice answered.

'Hi, Dad. Just calling to check you're ok.'

'Why wouldn't I be?'

'After the heart attack thing.'

'Better late than never, I suppose,' he muttered.

'It only happened on Saturday night.'

'Yes, three days ago.'

She drew in a breath. 'Well, sorry, but I don't get much reception here and I've been busy. This is the first time since then I've been in an area where I can make a call. I sent Ma messages.'

'She doesn't like messenger because she only gets it on her tablet and she hates using the thing.'

'Why don't you sign up for it then?'

'There's no point. Everyone living somewhere sensible can use the mobiles.'

Sensible? *Well, bugger me!* He was so set in his ways, nothing would ever drag him out of them. 'At least half of rural Britain doesn't get reception.'

'Nonsense, that's an urban myth.'

Holly rolled her eyes at her mirror. Thank Christ he couldn't see her. She was used to this. At least he was ok. Arguing was normal for him and he would argue black was white to prove himself right.

'So, what are you doing on that island?'

'I'm working.'

'Which brings me back to my other point. Why work in a place with no reception?'

'Because I'm not right in the head?' she mumbled to herself. 'Guess what, I saw the aurora borealis last night; it was amazing.'

'Don't change the subject. And I doubt that's what you saw. No one ever sees that, unless they know where to look. It's very rare. More likely to have been lights from an offshore windfarm.'

'No, Dad. I know what I saw. There aren't any offshore wind-farms near here anyway.'

'Did you get photographic proof?'

'No, but my neighbour did. He took photos on his phone; I could get him to send you them.'

'I don't want some random person sending me pictures. Who is this person? I need to write down their name and number before they send me anything.'

'His name...' Holly squirmed in her seat. This would crash through her dad's bubble like a lead brick. '...is Farid Al-Karim.'

'Pardon? And where does he come from?'

Holly groaned. Could she hang up and blame a reception blip? 'Daraa.' Her voice was hushed.

'The place in Syria?'

'Yup, the very same.'

'And this person is living next door to you?'

'Yes, Dad.'

'Have you seen his paperwork? Does he have a permit to be here?'

'Please, Dad. Don't start that. He's a refugee and he's been through hell. Yes, he has all the paperwork. He spent months imprisoned in hostels waiting for it.'

'Pah,' her dad said. 'Make sure you lock your doors at night.'

Holly almost laughed out loud. 'No one locks their doors around here. And Farid is one of the most trustworthy people I know. I couldn't ask for a better neighbour.' Or lover. Best her dad didn't hear that bit.

'I don't like the sound of that. Sounds like he's trying too hard. Next thing, he'll want to marry you.'

'What? Why would he do that?'

'He'll see you as a free pass to staying in the country.'

Holly gritted her teeth. 'Don't be ridiculous. Farid's great and that's all you need to know. I'm glad you're feeling better. Take care. I should go now. I've got lots of work to do.'

She ended the call and threw back her head. Dad could be so pig-headed, bigoted and bloody-minded. Sometimes there were flickers of a jolly side but they'd been squashed out of sight for years. If he could have excommunicated her after the Gavin fiasco, he would have. Her behaviour got her what she deserved in his eyes. 'I didn't act in a manner befitting a lady,' she said in a fake plummy voice. Not that he knew the truth of what had happened. Her cheeks heated and her skin crawled with cringy memories. They all thought Gavin had proposed to her and she'd turned him down. How could she tell them she was the one who'd brought it on herself? She'd misjudged Gavin's feelings completely and acted like a love-struck fool, thinking it would be cool to turn the tables and propose to him.

Honestly, her family were a piece of work. With her mother always resentful Holly hadn't been born with a penis and her father expecting her to be the pinnacle of ladylike decorum, she'd had a messed-up set of messages from an early age. 'Ah, to hell with it.' She was her own person now. What was her parents' approval worth anyway? Her father spent his life viewing the world through his tinted glasses. How could he ever understand Farid? From the comfort of his upgraded Victorian townhouse in Kelso, he'd have to renovate his Victorian beliefs before he could comprehend Farid's struggles. And how could Holly explain her feelings for him – when she couldn't wholly explain it to herself?

Throughout the afternoon, she worked on the Mardicon and Co. project, trying not to let her mind stray to Robyn's work. If she chased something new and shiny now, it would be harder to get back to this.

Engrossed in it, she only looked up from her screen when Farid's door banged shut. She set her laptop aside and jumped up. After the unsettling conversation with her dad, she wanted to hug Farid and remind herself everything was ok between them. The Christmas tree twinkled in the corner, and Holly smirked. She prised a long string of tinsel from it before she left. He wanted her to appreciate the magic of Christmas, so how about this?

A few steps down the path, then up Farid's brought her to his door. She rapped and waited.

He opened it and smiled. 'You can come in, any time. I don't mind.'

'I thought you might be in the shower. I didn't want to come in and freak you out.'

'No? Don't you want to come in and play?'

'Maybe I do.' She stepped into the hall, unravelled the tinsel and draped it over his neck, then pulled him close with it. 'I missed you today.'

'Same, *jamilati.*' He wrapped his arms around her waist and pulled her hips against his. 'I miss you every second.'

'Merry Christmas.' She rubbed against him, pressing her lips to his.

He kissed her deeply and smoothed his hands over her back, as though caressing a precious jewel. '*Bahebek, jamilati.*' He ran the tip of his nose down hers before sealing his mouth on hers again.

Holly sighed into the kiss. The tinsel vines bolstered the bond of love spiralling between her and Farid. She wanted more of this. The happiness in her chest, the solace of knowing someone was there for her. She'd had a version of this with Gavin but it had always been more clinical and planned. What she had with Farid was raw and exciting. Before she could stop herself, she was hauling off her shirt and starting on his buttons.

CHAPTER SEVENTEEN

Farid

'M*arhaba*, Mama.' Farid's eyes filled with tears as his mother's face appeared on his phone screen.

'Farid? I can see you.'

'Ah, Nadda, you're the best sister, getting this to work.'

'Of course I am,' she said off-screen. 'Everyone knows that.'

'Everyone except me,' Sadira said.

Farid grinned as his youngest sister muscled her way into the picture. 'You can both be the best for different things.'

'Stop the fighting, girls,' a deep voice said.

'Baba.' Tears leaked and Farid pressed his fingers to his lips. 'You're there too.'

'Yes,' his mama said, 'we're all here.'

'Hello, son. I'm pleased to see you're well.' His father's thick eyebrows rose in the middle and his lips twitched. 'You understood before all of us the danger. We should have listened.'

Farid's heart swelled. That was as good as an apology. 'I never meant to hurt you, Baba. Any of you.' He sniffed, swallowing salty water. 'I miss you all terribly and I love you all so much.'

His mama bobbed her head slowly. 'Farid. You're a good boy and we miss you too. You're ok though and safe, yes?'

'Yes. I'm safe here. It's very different.'

'Is it cold?' Sadira asked.

'Very. There's ice in the mornings but no snow yet. A man I work with says they don't get much snowfall on the island so I might not see it. Not this year anyway. But I saw the aurora borealis a couple of nights ago. That was spectacular.'

They nodded with wide eyes, glancing at each other.

'Are you all ok?' he asked.

His mama pulled a face. 'We get by. It's not the same as our old home, but we're lucky, I suppose. We got out in time. It makes me so sad when I think about what's happened to the old country.'

'I know, Mama.'

'Yes. It is not easy for anyone. We make the most of what we can, but it'll never be the same,' his father said. 'How is Archie?'

'He's good and always helpful.'

'I remember he was a very well-mannered young man,' Khalif said.

'He's married now. His wife's lovely too.'

'I'm happy to hear it.'

The front door clicked. 'Farid.' Holly's voice called from the hall and Farid scrunched up his face.

'Who's that?' his mama asked. Always sharp, she never missed a thing.

'Holly, my neighbour.'

'And she just walks in?' Nadda shared a look with Sadira, her dark eyebrows high on her forehead.

'Hush.' Farid glanced at the door. 'She's not just my neighbour, we're friends. Very good friends.'

'She's your girlfriend.' Sadira's mouth fell open.

'*Ay, na'am,*' Farid said, and his sisters started giggling and chattering.

Holly poked her head around the door and held her finger to her lips, mouthing, 'I didn't realise you were on the phone.'

'Farid,' his father said. 'It's unwise to have a girlfriend in Britain. Is she a British girl?'

'Yes, Baba.' He beckoned Holly over. She shook her head and held up her hands. Her long, windswept hair trailed over the shoulders of her white sweater.

'It isn't wise,' his father said.

'And what will happen if you come back?' his mama said.

'I can't come back any time soon, Mama. I'm sorry.' He tipped his head, spotting the disappointment flicker in her eyes. 'But let me introduce you to Holly. She really is a wonderful woman. You'll like her.'

'Aw man,' Sadira said. 'He's got it bad.'

'Or lost his mind.' Nadda keeled over laughing.

'Bet that's not all he's lost.'

'Girls!' barked Khalif – ha! Father formidable was back.

'Holly, it's my family.' He switched back to English, muting the sound. His father and sisters spoke some English. 'Come and say hi. They want to meet you.'

'You told them about me?'

'Yes,' He gave a little shrug.

'Seriously?'

He held out his hand. 'Come on, I'll translate.'

With a deep sigh, she sat beside him on the sofa. He unmuted the chat and beamed. 'Here she is, the wonderful Holly.'

'*Marhaba!*' They waved and smiled.

'*Marhaba.*' Holly briefly lifted her hand.

Farid gawped at her. 'You speak Arabic?' If she did, great... Except for the fact he'd been telling her he loved her for the past few days. Surely, she didn't know *that?*

'That's my limit.'

'She's beautiful,' his mama said. Mama always said kind words, even if she didn't think the idea was a good one. 'And her eyes are clever. I can see she is intelligent.'

'Is she from a good family?' his father asked.

Farid smiled. 'Mama thinks you're beautiful and intelligent.' His gaze lingered on her for a moment. 'And she's right. Baba wonders if you're from a good family.'

She shuffled in the seat. 'They're ok.'

'*Ay, na'am,* Baba,' Farid said to his father. 'They're good.'

'I hope you are happy together,' his mama said. 'I'd like one day to meet her for real but I don't suppose that will happen soon.'

Holly sat upright with her palms on her thighs as the conversation unfolded. Farid translated when appropriate. Tension radiated from Holly's rigid body. But this time with family was too precious. Maybe it would have been kinder to let her skip this, but bringing these two parts of his life together was important.

When sign off time came, he was as emotional as his mama. 'I love you all so much. Let's do this again soon.'

'Very soon, my boy, very soon.'

He hit the end call button and looked at his feet for a moment, filling his lungs with air, then slowly letting it go. Holly slipped her arms around his shoulders and held him. He counted six breaths, then rested his head on her. 'I miss them.'

'I know.' She rubbed her hand down his arm.

'I'm sorry if that was awkward. Being with you makes me happy. I wanted to share something good with them.'

'Farid.' Holly lowered her eyes. 'You make me happy too. I just don't want to get ahead of ourselves.'

He clutched her knee and steadied himself. 'No. I get that.' But he didn't really. Didn't she want to make the most of this? Shout about it? Go tell it on the mountain? He did and he would. But no. Her time here would end after Christmas and she wouldn't stay – not for him. He was from a different world. And right now, he wanted to go back to that world and fall into his mother's arms. She would tell him what to do. That luxury wasn't his anymore. He had to decide for himself. If that meant losing Holly in a few weeks, could he accept it? He had to.

'Sometimes life sucks.' He got to his feet and stomped to the kitchen area.

'I wish I could make things better.'

'You can't. So, don't try. Shall we eat?'

'Sure. I can help you with that.'

'Come on then.'

He pulled out a pot, filled it and lifted it onto the stove. Holly wrapped her arms around him from behind, leaning her head on his back and slipping her hands under his top. 'I can be here for you.'

'You can. For a little while anyway.'

And there was the rub. He better not get too used to this because like everything else in his life, it was about to be cut out and torn away.

Chapter Eighteen

Holly

Holly rested her chin on her hands, staring at the screen. No, no, please no. Not a crisis at three o'clock on a Friday. If she couldn't fix this, and fast, it would mean a weekend of work.

She tapped several keys and waited, clamping her lip between her teeth. Nothing happened. 'Oh, come on!' she yelled at it. 'Why won't you just work?'

Farid's door slammed shut and she held her breath momentarily. Since she'd crashed his chat with his family the other night, he'd been distant. Two nights alone, with him on the other side of the wall, was torturous. If she could just fix this damn glitch. Then she'd go round and see him. Check he was ok. His excuses of needing sleep because work was tough didn't wash. While it may be true, something wasn't right. Had talking to his family made him rethink? Had they persuaded him not to date her? Maybe they'd hated the look of her and his translations had been fake.

Code after code she keyed in, and still nothing happened. Her fingers moved like lightning. A knock on the door broke the cycle. Then it opened and closed.

'*Marhaba*,' Farid called.

'Hey.' Holly looked around as he came into the living room and teased her fingers through her hair, tossing it up so it fluffed over her shoulders.

'Are you ok?' He lowered his head, blinking his sparkling blue eyes.

'Yeah. I was going to come and see you later. I've missed you.'

'I'm sorry. Seeing my family again… It made me stop and think. But I missed you too. Now…' He arched an eyebrow suggestively. 'Close your eyes.'

'Why?'

'Please.'

Holly did it, trying not to peek, but sensed he'd moved closer. The warm scent of amber oil filled her nostrils.

'Now open.'

She flicked up her eyelids. He was behind her and when she turned, her gaze was drawn upward. A sprig of mistletoe dangled over her head. 'Seriously.'

Shaking the mistletoe, he pouted his lips and closed his eyes. She did the same, giving him a Charlie Brown style kiss. He chuckled.

'You didn't need that to get a kiss.' Holly eyed the mistletoe. 'In fact, I'll give you a better one if you get rid of it.' She returned to her screen and grimaced.

'Are you sure you're ok?'

'Yes. It's just work.' She hammered a key. 'Something's gone wrong with this bloody program.'

'What?' Farid grabbed the stool from the far side of the breakfast bar and pulled it up to sit beside her.

She threw some more lines of code at it. 'I'm debugging a program I've been developing, and something has gone wrong. I don't have time to go through it again and I don't want to ask Gavin to help.'

'Who's he?'

She let out a sigh. 'An ex. But also someone I used to work with a lot and I've been working with him again on this.'

'Oh yeah?'

'Purely work, Farid. I won't be going down any other route with him again. No danger. But he's really good at his job.'

'Ok.'

'I thought this would be a quick fix.'

'Can I see?' He shifted his seat closer, peering at the screen.

She frowned. 'Do you understand incremental program development?'

'Yes.'

'You do?'

He nodded. 'I told you, this used to be my job.'

'Go on then.' She pushed the laptop towards him.

'I might find nothing. But sometimes fresh eyes help.'

'Do you want a coffee?' She got to her feet and folded her arms, watching him lean forward to examine the data.

'Can I have a marvellous hot chocolate, please? I left a bag in the hall. It's full of stuff you might like.' He grinned as he stared at the screen, scrolling, then typing. His fingers moved like a superhuman.

Almost as fast as me. Nipping into the hall, Holly picked up the bag. Soon the contents were laid on the worktop. She scratched her forehead. Squirty cream, flakes, chocolate sprinkles and a miniature bottle of rum. *Seriously?*

'Rum in hot chocolate?'

Farid's smile grew but he didn't glance up from the screen. 'Why not? We only live once, huh?'

She took out a measuring jug and filled it with milk. 'I should look up a recipe. I haven't a clue what to do with the rum.' She pulled out her phone.

'Here. I've found it. I think.'

Holly almost dropped her phone and ran around behind him. She peered over his shoulder. 'Oh my god, it could be. Let's see.' He pushed the laptop back to her and she sat on the stool.

'Do you want me to fix it?'

'You know how?'

'Don't you trust me?' He quirked a grin.

'I do but I also trust you more with the hot chocolate; I don't trust myself with that.'

He laughed. 'Ok, you do the computer. I fix the drinks.'

With the right code isolated, Holly worked through it, debugging, and rewriting where necessary. Farid boiled milk in the pan and gorgeous aromas filled the room. Friday night was looking up again.

A hot chocolate with a perfect swirl of whipped cream landed on the worktop beside her in one of the fancy glass mugs she'd found in the cupboard – a masterpiece worthy of a barista in an artisan coffee shop. 'Mmm. I hope this tastes as good as it looks and smells.' She ran the new codes. Phew. All working. Delicious, sweet scents filled the room. 'I'm going to email this to the test team and get them to check it. Hopefully, that's it fixed. I honestly can't thank you enough.'

'No bother. It feels good to do it again.'

She closed her laptop. 'I'm done for the day and, thanks to you, the weekend is clear. Maybe tomorrow we should bake the Christmas cake.'

'Perfect.' He clinked his glass on hers. '*Fe Sehetak.*'

'*Sláinte.*' She sipped the drink. Cream crowned the tip of her nose. She crinkled it and crossed her eyes, pretending to look at it.

'Let me.' Farid rubbed it off with a quick stroke of his forefinger.

'Has it gone?'

'Missed a bit.' He leaned forward, pressing his lips to hers, sucking on her top lip. The bristles of his beard tickled her. 'Got it.'

'If you do that again, I won't finish it. I'd rather have you.'

'Later. We shouldn't waste this.'

'Yes. Let's not rush.'

'Does that mean we can watch Christmas movies tonight?'

'Oh, get a grip,' Holly said. 'I definitely won't last through one of them.'

But Farid's powers of persuasion were almost as good as his under-the-covers skills... and his barista skills, and his coding skills. Seriously, was there anything he couldn't do? Reluctantly Holly agreed to watch *A Christmas Carol*, on the strict instruction Farid wouldn't refer to her as a Scrooge afterwards.

Lying in his arms as he stroked her hair, kissed her and caressed her was distracting enough to make the film bearable.

'How about Mrs Scrooge?' he whispered.

'Shut up.'

He chuckled, rubbing his hand down the inside of her pyjama bottoms and teasing her thigh. Two could play at this game. She mirrored the move and he shifted, trying hard to keep his eyes on the TV, but she had his attention.

He groaned. '*Jamilati*, patience, please.'

'I told you before, that's not my best virtue.'

'Do you have any?' He smirked.

'No, I'm much better at sins. Wrath, greed, envy... lust.' She kept her eye on him as she spoke.

'Holly, stop it.' He clamped his hand over hers to prevent her from moving it. 'Let's watch the end. It's nearly done.'

She nuzzled into him. The end of the film couldn't come soon enough. The second the credits started rolling, she pounced on the remote and switched off the TV. Flinging the remote away, she straddled Farid's lap. 'Can I have you now?'

'I'm all yours, Mrs Scrooge.'

'Don't call me that.' She pushed his shoulders back, pinning him to the sofa.

He laughed. 'I love it when you talk like that, *jamilati*.'

She dipped in and kissed his neck. His skin was rough with stubble against her lips. 'You're such a hot bastard.' She continued up his neck and nibbled his earlobe.

Farid shifted underneath her, then wrapped his arms around her bottom, and she squealed. Then, to her shock, he pushed onto his feet, taking her with him.

'Christ, you're so strong.'

'You're like a twig,' he said. 'And I've been lifting logs all day. I promise you weigh nothing, *jamilati*.'

'Where are we going?'

'Bed.'

Wrapped in Farid's arms, Holly didn't want to move. His hot slab of a body beneath her was perfect, like he'd been cut to fit her exactly. And not just his physique, his soul was a perfect match for hers too. The physical pleasure of their encounters was intense but so much more was going on here. He sighed and his hands moved over her back; one grasped her shoulder and the other cupped her bottom.

'*Bahebek, jamilati,*' he whispered.

'Merry Christmas.' The words tripped off her tongue. *Hmm.* They weren't the ones she really wanted to say but they'd have to do. The others were... Well, no. She couldn't. She mustn't even think them.

'Holly.'

'Yes.'

'I must tell you something.'

With an effort, she prised herself off him and rolled onto the bed beside him. He grabbed the blanket and pulled it over them, pressing her against his hot skin.

'What is it?'

His chest rose and fell slowly. 'I had no other women before you.'

She glanced up but, in the darkened room, couldn't make out much of him.

'You were my first kiss, my first everything. That's why I was embarrassed on the beach. I messed up.'

'Oh, Farid.' She traced a heart shape on his taut pecs. 'I wouldn't have known. I kind of expected you wouldn't have been with anyone for a while.' It had been a while for her too. 'I mean, after what you've been through, it wouldn't have been surprising.'

'I don't want to disappoint you.

'You haven't. You're amazing and I don't just mean in bed. You're a great guy. Even the Christmas stuff is growing on me. It's like Farid's Christmas fun house.'

'I like that.' He stroked her hair. 'When I talked to my family, it took me back and made me wonder if I did the right thing. I just... I'm still finding my place and I don't want to hurt anyone or do wrong.'

'You've done nothing wrong.'

'I bet that woman on the beach thinks different.'

'Yeah, well. Never mind her. Busybody.'

He let out a laugh.

'But...' She huffed a sigh. 'Will being with me hurt your family? Don't they approve?'

'They know in their hearts I won't be back for a long time. Mama wants me to be happy; that's why she says you're beautiful and intelligent. She wants to like you. But Baba is not so sure. He's traditional about many things and he has an old way of thinking about women. I worry for my sisters. I hope one day they can have the freedom you have but I fear my father won't allow it.'

'Maybe he'll change.' Silly comment – like suggesting her own father would change his lifelong political views.

'I wanted to tell you. I owe you the truth.'

'Thank you.' She planted a soft kiss on his cheek and he turned his head to join in. His jaw worked under her hand as they kissed long and deep, stirring Holly to the core, not with lust but a profound sense of happiness and comfort.

When they broke off, she slowly circled his back with her palm as he held her close. His breathing slowed and deepened, and his grip slackened.

'Sleep well.' Her eyes wouldn't close; they stayed pinned open in the darkness. Normally, she'd go out like a light, especially after a sexy time like this. But her brain wouldn't shut down.

Farid's chest moved steadily and his warmth surrounded her in the silent night. Everything was still and serene. His confession was sweet. How hard must it be to confess to something like that? *Especially to someone like me.* A woman who'd had a few partners over the years. Everyone had to start somewhere, and after the life he'd had, it wasn't surprising. What was surprising was how good he was. But then, her own lust had played a part. She knew what she wanted and wasn't afraid to ask or show him. Maybe that had helped.

'Oh, god.' She stroked his shoulder and his strong upper arm. 'I hope I didn't force you into anything.'

No, he'd been as willing as her but another niggly thought popped up like a glaring orange streetlight amid a perfect starry night.

If she was Farid's first, then this was dangerous. He'd introduced her to his parents, and hoped his mum might meet her in the flesh one day. He had nothing to measure her against. Did he think the first woman who'd shown him attention must be the one and only? She couldn't have that. This wasn't meant to be serious. This was a fling. She didn't do long-term. Not now. Once she'd wanted nothing else but the Gavin fiasco had made up her mind for her. Now she was happy on her own. How could she make that clear without hurting Farid?

CHAPTER NINETEEN

Farid

Farid wiped flour from his brow and laughed. 'Seriously, Holly, you need baking lessons.'

'Me? I'm not the one covered in flour.' She folded her arms, innocently eyeing the bag she'd exploded over Farid. 'I hope you're not suggesting because I'm a woman I should know how to bake.'

'I would never.' He thrust up his hands. 'I like my body parts too much. I can't trust you not to cut something off if I say a thing like that.'

'You're not wrong.' She scanned down his body over the stripy butcher's apron they'd found in a drawer, and her eyes lingered below his waist. Her lips curled up. 'And that would be a pity because I like your body too.'

'I'm happy to hear it.' He measured the flour with a grin splitting his face. So far, so good. He'd confessed and she was ok with it. Making her happy was his mission, one he was enjoying too much to stop.

'I should have put on my Santa hat,' he said, 'and you could have worn the elf suit.'

'Don't even go there.'

'You would have been such a sexy little elf, *jamilati.*' He wrapped his arms around her and she squealed as he rubbed his floury hands up her sides and back.

'Farid, seriously. Look at me.'

'My greatest pleasure.'

'Oh, shut up.' She dusted herself off.

'Now, back to business. We must mix this, then add fruit.'

'Go for it, chef.'

Farid cracked the eggs and sifted in the dry ingredients. The rich aroma of spices filled the room. Mm... like Mama's kitchen. He pounded the mixture with the beaters, then opened the container of fruit they'd left to stew. 'Smells interesting.'

'I don't even like Christmas cake,' Holly said. 'It's overrated.'

'You will like this one.'

'Why?'

'Because it was made with love.'

'Good god.' She slapped her hand to her forehead. 'Sounds like it's your baby or something.'

Farid's cheeks burned but he smiled at her deflection. How quickly she batted away the idea of love.

'I've read that when we stir the cake, we make a wish.'

Holly shook her head. 'I can't do that.'

'Why not?'

'Just… I just don't want to.'

'Please.' What could possibly be stopping her from doing something as ordinary as stirring a cake? 'Look…' He put out his arm and guided her in front of him. With shuffling feet, she let him and he slipped his hands around her waist, holding her from behind. 'Shall I put it in?'

'I beg your pardon.'

'The fruit, Holly. You are naughty.'

'I know.' She chuckled. 'Let me do it.' She slid the fruit into the bowl. Farid lifted the wooden spoon, then gathered her hands beneath his. Together, they stirred the thick mixture.

'Now, make a wish, but don't say what it is. If you tell it doesn't work.' He closed his eyes, resting his chin on her shoulder and inhaling the sweet scent of her conditioner. Wishes flooded his brain. His family's safety, peace in his country and love. '*Bahebek, jamilati.*' He planted a kiss on her cheek. *And I wish you would stay with me forever.*

'Merry Christmas,' she muttered.

'Let's get this in the tin, then we can bake it. It takes four hours.'

'Oh, well. Plenty of time to do something else then.'

'Exactly.'

'First up, I need to shower. I'm covered in flour. Coming?' She arched her eyebrow.

'Are you kidding?' Was she? She was one hundred per cent attractive and scorched his blood with her talk, but she was also terrifying.

'Not kidding. You look like you need a good scrub to me.'

How could he refuse? He set the cake to bake and followed her towards the bathroom.

An hour later, Farid was well washed after the hottest shower in heaven or hell. He had nothing to compare her with but this had to be the most intense initiation a man could have – no complaints.

Holly strolled into the living area, sweeping her long hair into a ponytail, and smiled from ear to ear. Farid leaned his head on his hand on the sofa arm. 'So much for a relaxing weekend. You tire me out.'

'I don't believe a word of it. I mean, what age are you? Twenty-nine? Thirty?'

'Ha. No. Twenty-six.'

'Twenty-six?' Holly gaped, still holding her hands behind her head as she fixed her hair.

'Yup. Why?'

'Because I'm thirty-two.'

He fiddled with the cuff of his sweater. 'Does it matter? My father is seven years older than my mother.'

'Yeah, it never seems quite so bad when it's the man who's older.'

'Holly, Holly, I never thought I'd hear you saying something like that. If I said it, you'd string me up or cut my bits off.'

She laughed. 'True. And it's not like...' Her gaze dropped and she looked away. 'Well, you know.'

'No. What do you mean?'

'Nothing. Listen, I need to go to Tobermory. I haven't bought food for over a week. I've been so distracted with work and you.'

'Sorry.'

'I don't mind. It's just I need supplies. I won't be too long hopefully. Will you stay and mind the cake?'

'Of course, *jamilati*, I do anything for you. You know that.'

'Thanks, gorgeous.'

He got to his feet and opened his arms.

She hugged him.

'Take care.'

'I will.' She planted a chaste kiss on his cheek before she left.

He slumped on the sofa. What to do now? Things he'd enjoyed in Syria seemed far removed from this life. He used to swim and play tennis, but his racket was long gone. He didn't have a computer and his phone had limited capacity for entertainment. Maybe listen to some more Christmas music?

As he considered returning to his cottage and getting a book, a knock came on the door. He jumped up and hurried through, pulling it open. 'Hello, Georgia.'

'Oh, hi, Farid.' She furrowed her brow a little. 'Can I come in? I need to speak to Holly.'

'Sure, come in, but she's not here.'

'Isn't she? Then why are you here?' She made her way into the hall, carrying a large bag.

'We have a cake in the oven.'

Georgia raised an eyebrow. 'An actual cake or do you mean she's…' Georgia pushed her hand from her chest to her midriff, making the shape of a large belly.

'No, no, not that. A real cake. A Christmas cake. It's baking. I have to watch it in case the house burns down.'

'Phew, you had me worried for a minute there. So, where is she?'

'She's gone to Tobermory for shopping.'

'Hmm.' Georgia checked her watch. 'I have to get to the shop but I have a major favour to ask her. She probably won't do it but I'm desperate.'

'What is it?'

'I need someone to be our elf for a couple of hours tomorrow.'

Farid put his fingers to his lips and shook his head. 'She won't do that. No way. She will kill you first.'

'Yeah, I thought that. I'm not sure what to do. I've asked everyone but no one can do it. I can't do it myself because I have to watch the shop. We've got a tour group coming in and Autumn can't do it; she's struggling with morning sickness or all-day sickness as she's calling it. We can't have Santa's elf puking on the kids.'

'I'm sorry. I'm sure she'll say no. If you want a man-elf, I'll do it.'

'I'd let you, but there's no way you'll fit the costume. You're skinny enough but you're a bit too...' She dropped the bag, made a fist and flexed an imaginary bulging bicep.

'Yeah, sorry. I have PJs I could wear but they are in the wash. I must dry them first.'

'Hmm. That can be the reserve plan, as long as they're not too revealing. We don't want the mums fainting.'

'What?'

'Never mind. I don't suppose you could use your charm on Holly.' Georgia smiled. 'You have a way with her.'

'*Ya lahui.*' He slapped his cheek. 'You are joking? She's already threatened to remove parts of my body this morning.'

'Oh-kay.' Georgia glanced from side to side. 'The two of you have an interesting relationship.' She checked her watch again. 'I should go. I'd appreciate it if you dry those jammies just in case and if you have any luck with Holly, let me know, but don't endanger yourself.'

'I lock the knives away.'

'That kind of thing.'

'Are you sure you want her as an elf?'

'Not really, but she's literally the last person on the island I've asked, apart from Carl's aunt Jean who's in her nineties, though knowing her she'd probably do it.' She picked up the bag and handed it to Farid. 'There's the costume if she's up for it. It's only for two hours between one and three and it'd be a lifesaver if she can do it.'

Farid shook his head as Georgia left. So far he'd sweet-talked Holly into all sorts of Christmas capers but surely this was a step too far. He eyed the bag with the costume in it and experienced a hefty sense of déjà vu.

Chapter Twenty

'Absolutely no,' Holly said. 'Have you lost your mind? Has Georgia? Why can't she do it herself? Can't Archie mind the shop for two hours and she could be the elf? Or I'll mind the bloody shop and she can do it.'

'It's ok, *jamilati*.' Farid took both her shoulders in his hands and held her steady. 'She said *if* you could. You don't have to. No one will make you. I can be the man-elf in my PJs.'

She broke away and rubbed her forehead. 'If I don't, I'll feel really bad. Ugh. When we were at uni, Georgia and I had a summer job where we dressed up as court jesters and did silly displays for kids at a local castle. But this...'

'So she knows you can do it.'

'It was over ten years ago. I've grown inhibitions since then.'

'Ha! No, you haven't. You can't say that to me, not after—'

'Yeah, ok.' She threw out her hands. 'But in some ways, I have. And I've also developed an aversion to children.'

Farid cocked his head. 'Why? They're so important.'

'I'm just an old cynic.'

'Nonsense.' He pushed his fingers into Holly's hair and drew her face close.

Oh no, if he kissed her, she'd melt and do every bloody thing he asked.

'If you do this, *jamilati,* I would like to help undress the naughty elf after.'

'Farid...!' She gritted her teeth as he gently kissed her neck.

'I wear my Santa hat... and nothing else.'

'Oh, good god. Do you think it's a good idea for me to have thoughts like that rattling through my head while I'm trying to stop kids screaming at Santa for two hours?'

'Come on, I do it with you.'

'Seriously? Are you going to sit on the rug in your Santa hat and your birthday suit? You'll have all the mothers queuing up to see that.'

'Haha. No. I wear my lumberjack shirt over my PJs.'

'You'd make more money with the mothers than I will with the kids.'

'Does that mean you're doing it?'

'It appears I have no choice.'

Holly grimaced at her reflection. When Farid dropped this costume at her feet a couple of weeks ago, she should have picked it up and hurled it into the ocean or burned the hideous thing.

Instead, she was now roped into the tight Lycra looking like a cross between Diana Rigg in *The Avengers* and Will Ferrell in his Buddy suit.

'Oh, *jamilati*.' Farid poked his head around the door. 'Sexiest elf ever.'

'Not helpful.' She turned herself in the mirror. Her build was athletic and she was blessed with a reasonably flat bottom and stomach. Her hips were wide and her breasts a little too large to pull off the classic elfin style. 'I already look more like I'm on the game than going to the grotto.'

'You're stunning. No matter what you wear.'

His words were always beautiful, his proficiency in English remarkable. His talents were boundless and shouldn't be wasted by circumstances – or squashed by a bad relationship. He was only twenty-six and she was his first love. If she could make things good, maybe they could part on reasonable terms and he could go into the world with confidence and find someone more suited to him.

A tide of nausea ripped through her. Farid with someone else! No. *He's mine.* And she'd scratch out anyone's eyes if they tried to steal him from her. *Stop this.* She had to if they were going to part ways without her going crazy.

The house still smelt amazing from their cake baking the day before. Now they had a perfect cake ready for icing. Another wave of sickness crashed in Holly's stomach; the creeping sense of humiliation when she remembered the last time she'd decorated a Christmas cake.

She grabbed her coat and hauled it on. 'This costume doesn't give me much room to manoeuvre.' She adjusted the leggings.

Farid drove her to Georgia's quaint little boat shop. Holly hadn't visited it yet. Behind the shop was another structure, like a shed, with an enormous sign reading Santa's Grotto. The eaves dripped with fairy lights set on a cycle likely to induce an epileptic fit.

In the car park area, Farid pulled up beside a minibus with a picture of a sea eagle and the name Hidden Mull emblazoned on the side.

'Seriously?' Holly said. 'There's a tour bus here? Are they shipping hundreds of kids from the mainland especially for this?'

'I don't know,' Farid said. 'Georgia said she had a tour coming in. That's why she wants to be in the shop.'

How had she got herself into this? She got out of the car, keeping her head down. *Please, ground, open and remove me from this hell.* Even if it took her straight to another one, because, right now, she fancied her luck more with Satan than Santa. Anyone who didn't know she had on an elf costume under her coat would think her someone with a lurid taste in leggings. 'What am I supposed to do now?

'We find Georgia.' Farid took her hand and led her through the quirky mullioned doors fitted perfectly into the upturned boat hull that made the frame of the shop.

'Holly!' Georgia pounced on her before she'd got two feet into the shop. 'I can't thank you enough for this, really.'

'Yeah, you owe me big time. Why doesn't Archie mind the shop? Then you can be the elf.'

'He would have but we have a house party arriving in the main house and he's meeting them, so he can't.'

Holly skimmed around the shop. The nautical theme continued inside with driftwood shelves, nets hanging from the ceiling and fishing baskets full of handmade goodies. Holly wasn't as deeply into this kind of thing as Georgia but it was well done, tasteful and appealing. Some other people milled around, checking out the wares.

'And here's Kirsten.' Georgia pulled over a young woman with long, dark, curly hair. 'She was a bridesmaid at my wedding, but in case you've forgotten each other. And this is Kirsten's fiancé, Fraser.'

'I do remember.' Holly shook hands with a fit guy in a kilt. 'You do the island tours, don't you?'

Farid moved closer. Holly smirked. Was he jealous? Threatened?

'Yes, we do. And today we have the golden generation of Mull residents.' Fraser's smile was cute, the way his teeth grazed his lower lip. But he didn't set Holly alight in the way Farid did. The way only Farid could.

She scanned over the sea of people. 'You mean the pensioners?' A high proportion of older people were browsing the shop.

'Yup. My nan's here with her chums.'

'And are they coming to Santa's grotto?'

'No.' He grinned. 'We've finally convinced my nan and her friend to go up in the seaplane.'

'Fraser flies it.' Kirsten tossed him a proud grin.

'So cool,' Holly said.

Farid made an impatient sound behind her.

'I hope he knows what he's doing,' one of the elderly ladies said.

'Yes, Nan, I definitely do.'

'He used to fly Typhoons in the RAF,' Georgia said.

Holly turned to Farid and winked. His upper lip hooked slightly as he glanced around, a little too deliberate in the way he avoided Fraser's eyes.

'You remember Blair?' Georgia asked.

'Who?' Holly said.

'You met him at my wedding too.' Georgia waved to a young man with long blond dreadlocks. He was hand in hand with an elegant woman with her hair in a high afro updo. They were helping a lady with white fluffy hair to choose something.

Blair waved and got the attention of the two women.

'Oh, yes.'

'This is my friend, Holly,' Georgia said to the old lady.

'Lovely to meet you,' the old lady said.

'This is Mary, Rebekah's aunt.' Georgia smiled at Blair's partner. 'Is that right?'

'It's more complicated than that,' Blair said. 'Cousins twice removed or something.'

'That always sounds strange though,' Rebekah said.

'Aunt will do fine,' Mary said.

'And this is Farid,' Georgia said. 'And you've met Blair already.'

Holly half-rolled her eyes. Was Georgia going to introduce her to the whole island? 'So, what am I to do?'

'Two minutes and these guys will be on their way, then I'll sort you out and introduce you to Santa.'

'Great.'

Georgia either missed or ignored the sarcasm.

'She tried to rope me into doing the elf,' Kirsten said, 'but we already had this tour planned. I'm glad she found someone else.'

'Yeah,' Holly said. 'A piece of luck, that.'

'Are you going on this trip too?' Farid asked Blair.

'Yes,' Blair said. 'I've always wanted to go up in the plane.'

'And they're keeping me company,' Mary said. 'They're my family now. Wonderful pair, so they are.' She patted Blair, then Rebekah on the arm in turn.

This was all lovely, but could they get on with it?

Eventually, Georgia led Holly and Farid to the grotto.

'Hello, Santa.' Georgia swung open the door and beamed.

'Ho, ho, ho,' said a man with a shiny red face and a real bushy white beard.

'I have an elf and a lumberjack to help you today.'

'Great stuff.' Santa rocked in his chair, patting a fake round belly. The interior of the shed was like a cosy haven in a winter wonderland. Seriously? What was she doing here?

'And what's your name?' Santa asked.

'Farid.' He nudged Holly.

'What?'

'Holly, her name's Holly.'

'Holly.' Santa chuckled. 'The perfect name for my elf.'

'Funny,' she said. 'And what's your name?'

'Santa!'

Georgia and Farid laughed. 'Iain Beaton is his name,' Georgia said. 'Beatie, as everyone calls him... When they're not calling him Santa.'

This was more like the Halloween house of horrors than Santa's grotto. Why the hell were they all so jolly? Holly whipped off her coat and Georgia hung it on the coat stand in the corner. Farid wolf whistled.

Holly threw him the daggers as Georgia grinned.

'So, there are different bags,' Georgia said, 'with presents for different age groups. Your job is to find out what age the kids are when they come in, then hand Beatie the right one to give each child. That would be awesome.' She bustled over and adjusted a string of lights on the wall.

Farid put one arm around Holly's shoulder and whispered in her ear. 'You're the brightest star in the room. Smile and we smile too. Shine and we glow in your light.'

She made to pull a face at him but his expression was so sincere and intense. Did she really mean so much to him? This was getting way too deep.

'Is everyone ok then?' Georgia backed towards the door. Beatie and Farid nodded.

Holly followed Georgia to the door and stepped outside the shop with her. She shivered. It was arctic now she'd removed her coat. 'As I'm doing this as a favour, will you do something for me?'

'Sure, name it.'

'Give some of the proceeds of this to the refugees from Syria. They're not all as fortunate as Farid.'

Georgia patted Holly's upper arm. 'Absolutely. I couldn't agree more.' A queue had formed. Georgia waved to the first family and called, 'Come and see me in the shop after. Show me what you get from Santa, assuming you've behaved yourself this year, Beth.'

'Don't I always?' a tall, dark-haired woman replied. She'd been a bridesmaid for Georgia too. If Holly hadn't downed so much wine that day, she might remember more.

A smartly dressed man with his hair pulled back into a neat man-bun held his fist to his mouth and coughed. 'Ahem, right.'

He was her husband. Memories were returning. Not a bad looking guy.

The tall woman eyeballed him, a tiny smirk playing at the corner of her lips.

Holly welcomed them inside. 'And who do we have here?'

'This is Jack and Lucy,' the man said. 'They're our nephew and niece.'

'Ho, ho, ho, hello,' Beatie said.

'Uncle Murray, is that really Santa?' Lucy said.

'It looks like him,' Murray replied.

'And what age are Jack and Lucy?' Holly said.

'Jack's eight and Lucy's six.'

'Great. Well, if the two of you would like to go talk to Santa, we'll sort your presents. She plastered on her smile as she approached Farid. He'd already pulled out two presents from the sacks. She took them and stood by Beatie as he chatted to the kids.

Murray and Beth hovered by the door. He put his arm around her shoulder and whispered something. Holly looked away. Why did people have to be so happy? And show off about it? She hitched up her smile again. Jeez, she was a right Mrs Scrooge after all.

Jack and Lucy skipped out with presents, chatting and giggling with their uncle and aunt. Holly was in danger of contracting lockjaw as the next family appeared. This had to be overkill, right? Two couples came in with a bouncy round baby in a blue all-in-one suit. The man carrying him had to be his dad – same rosy cheeks.

'And who do we have here?'

'This is Angus,' the dad said.

'And what age is he?'

'Six months,' the mum said.

'Ho, ho, ho, hello, little man,' Beatie said.

'Is it ok if I take pictures?' the other man asked.

'I think so,' Holly said.

'Calum's his godfather,' the dad said. 'And likes to do everything right.'

Calum pulled out his phone as the mum and dad took Angus towards Beatie.

'Baby's first Christmas,' Farid whispered, handing Holly a present. 'It's something to celebrate.'

Holly held the present and waited. At the door, Calum had his phone poised. The pretty blonde woman beside him snatched it and re-angled it, pulling him in for a quick selfie. Holly looked away. *Here we go again.* Lovey-dovies everywhere. The mum, dad and Angus were cuddling and laughing beside Santa and this time Calum got the snap. They thanked Beatie and left. The blonde woman put her hand behind Calum and slipped it into the back pocket of his jeans.

Holly rolled her eyes. 'Get a room,' she muttered. Ha. She was a fine one to talk, after the way she'd carried on with Farid over the last few weeks.

Time ticked by in much the same way. Two screamers followed, then a girl who wouldn't come in at all. At two o'clock, Holly had almost had enough.

'One hour to go,' Farid whispered as a family left.

Holly welcomed the next group. 'And who have we here?'

'This is Rowan,' his mum said.

'And how old are you?' Holly asked.

'Nine.' He frowned at Santa.

'Would you like to talk to Santa?'

'Ho, ho, ho, hello!' Beatie said. Did he hear those words in his sleep? They'd haunt Holly for the rest of the week.

Rowan shook his head. 'That's not Santa. I'm too big. I know it isn't.'

What the hell to say? Her jaw hurt from pulling this cheery face. He was right. She'd felt the same way throughout her childhood. A friend of her sister had shattered the myth when she was eight and her parents hadn't bothered to carry it on after that. The mystery died and presents became things stuffed in stockings or shoved under the tree, forgotten about a few hours after they were opened. Would it have been any different if she'd believed for longer? She doubted it. When she'd been serious with Gavin, she'd tried to make Christmas something special. His family was into it big time. But she'd misjudged his intentions completely and their last Christmas together was the festive disaster to top them all.

'Would you like to shake hands?' Beatie said.

Rowan shook his head again.

'Hey,' Farid said. 'What do you like doing?'

Rowan frowned.

'He loves football,' his mum said. 'My daughter, Carys, she's much older than Rowan, is engaged to a footballer, Troy Copeland. You might have heard of him. Rowan loves to play with Troy.'

'That's great,' Farid said. 'Ah, I remember; he switched on the lights at the carol singing.' He handed a present subtly to Holly and crouched in front of Rowan. 'I tried football a long time ago. I was never very good.'

Rowan shrugged. 'I'm quite good.'

'I'm sure you are. Can I tell you something?' Farid continued. 'Ok.'

'I help today because I want to learn about Christmas. I come from Syria; it's far away and only a few people celebrate Christmas. I find it confusing. So, I understand it's hard for you. But you must trust your heart. Believe what's inside you. You believe in yourself and your skill at football. Do you believe in fun?'

'Well, yeah,' Rowan said, as though it was obvious.

'And will getting a present be fun?'

'I guess.'

'And do you believe in love?'

'Yuck,' Rowan said. His mum and dad shared a look.

'Maybe, but your parents love you and you love them, I'm sure. And by bringing you here, they want to show you love. What I've learned about Christmas so far is not the importance of Santa or cakes or trees, but joy, family and love.' He glanced up and caught Holly's eye. Her heart skipped a beat. This was getting worse. 'So, will you come say Merry Christmas to Santa?'

'Ok,' Rowan said.

Holly passed the present to Beatie.

'In Syria, we say, *Eid milad sa'id* for Merry Christmas. Can you say that?'

'Ed... *milad...*' Rowan said, '...sy... yeed.'

'Very good.'

Holly frowned. That didn't sound like the words he kept saying to her.

'You've definitely earned a present this year, young man,' Beatie said. 'After all that football training. Well done and have a very Merry Christmas.'

Farid winked at Holly. In a couple of weeks, she'd grown too fond of that face. The danger intensified. She was falling so fast for Farid a crash landing was imminent.

CHAPTER TWENTY-ONE

Farid

Farid pulled open the Velcro on the back of Holly's costume and prised it down, revealing her smooth back. She held her hair over one shoulder as he slipped off the Lycra.

'I forgot to say.' He breathed a gentle kiss onto her neck and slid his palms along her bare shoulder blade. She moaned. That noise. It bulleted lust straight to his core. 'I have an invitation to a party. Georgia gave it to me. Would you come with me?'

Holly let out a groan, stepped out of his grip and pulled off the remaining top half of the elf. 'She gave me one too. I'm not keen.' She grabbed a t-shirt and pulled it on. *Ah, ok.* So this undressing wasn't going any further. Curse his desperate body. He was ready. Without ceremony, Holly ripped off the stripy leggings and put on a pair of pyjama bottoms.

'Are you ok?' he asked.

'Don't you want to ice the cake?'

'I do, but you seem sad. What's wrong?'

She slumped onto the bed. 'You and me.'

'How is that wrong?' He blinked. 'I can leave if you want.'

'No, I don't. That's the problem. I like you being here. I like you.'

'That's good, isn't it?'

'No.' She threw up her hands. What was he missing? Where was she going with this? 'I'm not staying here, Farid. I like my life as it is. This is fun and… diverting. It's giving me company in a lonely place and making Christmas, well, almost fun. But it doesn't mean I'm sticking around.'

Farid thrust his hands into his back pockets and stared at the floor. 'I know that. You said before.'

'And I'm saying it again because I'm frightened.'

'Of me?'

'Of course not. But of where you might think this is going. I don't want to hurt you. I understand you haven't had a relationship before and you're all the more amazing for it, but I'd hate you to pin too much importance on this. Don't lose your heart over me. I want us both to know exactly where we stand.'

'Sure. I get it.' The words flowed from his lips. Lies. He didn't get it. Not really. He understood what she was saying but didn't she attach any value to this at all? Would it be that easy to throw him over when the time came? Not for him. She might be able to cast him aside, but his heart would suffer. This may be his first love but it was all-consuming and precious. If he hadn't been so drawn to her, he'd have kept his distance. Maybe he should have done anyway. Was his soul about to be shredded?

'Good.'

'Should I go, *jamilati*?'

'No. If we're on the same page, then stay.'

'Sure.' He couldn't waste a second with her: they were numbered. Each one must be cherished.

She didn't meet his gaze. 'Let's do this cake then and get it over with.'

Yes, get it over with. That was all it was to her. Something to be done quickly and pushed out of the way. 'Ok.' He sat beside her and put his arm around her shoulder. 'I hope you enjoy it too. I didn't suggest any of these things to upset you. They were things for us to do together and enjoy. Life is too short and valuable to waste. These little things are moments of joy – if we let them.'

Holly looked away and covered her mouth. 'God, don't, Farid. You'll make me cry and I hate crying; it's an ugly mess.'

'Nothing about you is ugly.' Maybe just one thing – her determination to be alone. She yielded into his arms, not crying, but slumped. The tip of his nose touched her hair and he dotted gentle kisses across her ear, her cheek, her neck. 'Come to the party with me, please. Let's make the most of the time we have together.'

'Ok.' She clasped his knee and squeezed. For a few moments they sat, just cuddling, and warmth poured into Farid's soul. Many moments had passed in his life he would rather forget but now he was saving these seconds with Holly. He never wanted to forget this feeling.

When they finally got to the cake, it was therapeutic rolling out the marzipan, then the icing and fitting it to the lumpy cake, leaving a perfectly smooth surface to work on. While Farid trimmed the edges, Holly sat at the breakfast bar with the trimmings, hunched over, moulding it and prodding it with a cocktail stick.

'What are you making?'

'It's a log.'

Farid leaned over and squinted. 'That's great.'

'Is it? Years ago, I used to make things with FIMO. I loved it but I don't have time anymore. This is the same idea.'

'What's FIMO?'

'It's like modelling clay that comes in different colours. It was all the rage when I was little.'

'You have a talent.'

'Thanks. So, I have a log and an axe. That's to symbolise you. The lumberjack.'

He grinned. 'Then I will make holly.' He sat opposite her and rolled some tiny balls. 'And a heart. It tells me Holly and Farid made this cake with love.'

She glanced up and half-narrowed her eyes.

'Because remember, *jamilati,* Christmas is about love, family and joy.'

'You should know better. Western Christmas commercialism has sucked you in.'

'Maybe it has, but this is my home now.' Like it or lump it, he had to accept it. Acceptance came easier with enjoyment. His heart had been filled with resentment when he was forced out of his homeland, but each little thing he tried and enjoyed lowered his stress levels. What would happen once Holly left? Already since her arrival, he'd got back so much of his old self and he wanted to keep it like that. No more upheaval required. But more was looming, whether he liked it or not.

'That's not a good argument, Farid.' She picked up her mini log and examined it. 'You don't always have to fit in and becoming too attached to a place is never a good idea.'

'I don't want to change myself but to make peace with what I have. I want to understand the culture, not lose who I am, but I work better in the place if I know how it works.'

Holly rested her chin on her hands. 'You'll easily manage that. You have a way with people.'

'Thank you, *jamilati*. And I don't mean to attach myself to a place, but I want to find things to love in a place so I can enjoy my home even if it isn't forever.'

'That's more sensible because nothing lasts forever. People change, priorities change. Things you thought you once wanted aren't important anymore.'

'I agree.' Though she clearly didn't extend that way of thinking to him. They placed their decorations on top of the cake and Farid covered it carefully with cling film. He lifted it to the far side of the worktop under the upper units, where it was coolest. As he stepped back to admire it, Holly's arms wrapped round him from behind.

'Let's go to bed,' she said.

'At six o'clock?'

'Why not? We missed a trick earlier.'

No more persuasion needed. They resumed their position on the bed where they'd been a couple of hours before. Holly's words still rung in his ears. She was leaving. Would a more experienced man walk away right now? How could he relinquish one moment with Holly? He'd missed out on every kind of love for so long. He wouldn't refuse it now but bank it and store it in reserve for empty times ahead.

She cuddled into him as they ran their hands over each other and he kissed her hair, pulling her as close as he could. *'Bahebek, jamilati.'*

'Merry Christmas to you too.' She nuzzled his neck. 'Though that isn't what you said to that boy. You said something completely different for Merry Christmas to him.'

Rumbled! He kissed her some more, lolling back on the bed and taking her with him. 'You can work it out for yourself.'

'Oh, I will.' She straddled him and raked her fingers into his hair. Wildfire rampaged through him. 'And if I find it's something naughty, I'll make you pay.'

He clamped his hands around her bottom and pinned her close. Maybe she'd be furious when she found out, but he still meant it and that wouldn't change any time soon.

Chapter Twenty-Two

Holly

Holly stood at the door, staring into the darkness. The cold air bit her face. She hugged herself. What was she doing here? When the fluff was swept away, what was left? She'd come to escape Christmas and hurtled headfirst into a festive nightmare.

Now she didn't just have Christmas to worry about, she also had Farid. 'Oh, god.' She rested her forehead on the doorframe. For a place so close to the edge of the world, it was both lonely and wonderful. And most of the wonderful happened when Farid was nearby. She craved him too much. He came home to her every night. They cooked together, had fun together, talked together, made love together and everything was a bit too perfect. What was to stop her from keeping it going?

She was supposed to be getting ready for the party but her head ordered her not to. Going somewhere public with Farid was making their relationship more than it should be. Come January, she was out of here and Farid would be nothing but a happy diversion she'd had one December. Staying here long-term wasn't a viable option. Or was it? At one time in her life, she'd wanted to take the settling-down road and spectacularly fucked it up. It had been her dream for so long. She'd been the girl who dreamed of a white wedding and all the trappings, but when it came to the crunch... Ugh. She covered her face, blotting out the memory. What a prize mess she'd made of things. Men weren't necessary for happiness. They could be good company but not in the long run. Everything that had happened post-Gavin had been better. She'd been freer and happier than ever before. Until now.

With a sigh, she closed the door and returned to the warmth of the cottage. She slumped onto the cosy sofa and hugged one of the reindeer cushions. This agonising was exactly what she was trying to avoid. Relationships did this. They brought self-doubt and uncertainty. No way did she need them in her life again.

A thud next door made her sit up. Was that Farid home? She'd just missed him. Somehow she had to tell him she couldn't go, but how could she break the news without breaking his heart? She couldn't face the look in his eyes when their end day came.

She sat upright on the sofa, unable to move. Run away? But where? Maybe if she stayed still, no one would find her.

'Holly!' Farid's voice called at the same time as the door opened.

'Shit.' She was still in her pyjamas.

He strolled into the living room and her eyes almost popped out of their sockets. He was always well-groomed but he'd gone all out. His beard was neatly trimmed and every curl of his hair worked in perfection with its neighbour. He tugged back the cuffs of a slick white shirt tucked into shapely black jeans.

'Wow.'

'This?' He glanced down and dusted an imaginary speck from his trouser leg. 'I borrowed this shirt from Archie. He says I can keep it but I won't need it again soon.' His gaze travelled over her and she sucked on her lip. What now? Could she turn him away when he'd made such an effort? Was she that heartless? 'You're not dressed yet?'

'I can't.'

He furrowed his brow, stepped towards her and sat down. 'Why not, *jamilati*?'

The utterly divine aroma of amber oil tickled her nostrils. His slightly open shirt presented his glorious chest – so kissable.

'Are you sick? I can stay here and look after you if that's better?'

'No. I'm fine. It's just...'

'Christmas?'

'Partly.'

Farid took her hand and gently stroked it. 'Why do you hate it so much?'

'The commercialism gets me. My family have always been materialistic. We had a lot of money growing up and my parents got me everything I wanted.'

'Then you're lucky.'

'No, because it had no meaning. There was no magic. It wasn't fair and it wasn't right. I grew up entitled, thinking I could have whatever I wanted, but my parents' gifts always came at a price. I wasn't what they wanted. A son.'

'And this makes you hate Christmas?'

Holly threw back her head. 'Not really. Things changed because of Gavin.'

'Your ex?'

'Yup. He was like me in so many ways. We had lots in common: we worked in the same field, the same company for a while, and had similar interests. I knew he was the guy for me.'

Farid dropped his gaze to his shoes.

'And he still is, huh?'

'No. Not at all. I wasn't what he wanted.' She rubbed at her forehead. 'I made a big mistake. I didn't think to ask him what he wanted. I assumed he wanted the same as me.'

'Which was?'

'A traditional family life. Big white wedding, a nice house, kids, two cars and a family holiday to Corfu every year.'

'You wanted that?'

'Yup. And I was sure he did too. His parents were like that so it seemed a reasonable assumption. They were Christmas freaks and very well-to-do; they own a chain of whisky distilleries. So I decided one Christmas, it was time to get engaged.'

'You decided?'

'I did. I thought it would be a fun idea if I proposed to him, and better still, if I did it in front of all his family at Christmas dinner. I thought they'd be thrilled and then I could tell my parents I'd reversed the roles, bagged Gavin as my husband and prove I was as good as any son.'

'Ah, *jamilati*, I guess none of this worked?'

'Nope. It was an epic fail. Oh, god. Worse even than epic. I baked a Christmas cake, like the one in there. I made a wish, and you can guess what that was.'

'That you and Gavin lived happily ever after?'

'Exactly. I iced it and put little treasures on top of it. One of them was a box with Gavin's name on it. I put a ring in the box with a slip of paper, saying *will you marry me?* Then I made sure after dinner he got the right piece.' She paused and stared at Farid. 'Can you see where this is going?'

'He said no.'

She lifted one shoulder in a half-shrug. 'He didn't have to. His face said it all. He asked for a private word and we went into the kitchen. He said he had no idea I was that serious and he needed time. That was when I realised what an idiot I'd been. His parents were horrified I'd done something so ridiculous, spoiled the evening and humiliated myself and everyone else in the process. I never told my family the truth. They think he proposed to me and I said no. I just hate it so much. It's so humiliating.'

Farid put his arm around her and gathered her into his chest. The gorgeous scent of his aftershave calmed her. 'This was a horrible thing to happen. But it's over and you are strong.'

'When I hear Christmas music and see the trees, it reminds me of the effort I poured into the surprise only for it to backfire.'

'Not just effort, *jamilati,* love. You offered this man your love and he chose not to take it. Maybe it was best. Your love wasn't wasted.'

Farid released her, then fell to his knees in front of her, placed his hands on her thighs and gazed up at her.

'What are you doing?' *He better not think about reversing the trick on me.* What the hell would she say? Could she pull a Gavin on him? How was that remotely fair after what she'd just told him? *Must get away.*

'Come with me tonight, please. Not because of Christmas. Christmas is a bad name for something good; it doesn't tell the whole story. What you celebrate here isn't just the birth of Christ, it's so much more. It's about celebrating the beauty of the land in winter when everything is cold and miserable; people, family, kindness, sharing and giving. It's about love. One day, you and I will be old and look back at this Christmas. The one where we learned about love.'

The drumming in Holly's chest hit fever point. The *L* word. She swallowed and took Farid's hands, raising them from her thighs. 'You're right. You always find the right words. I'll get ready.'

She stood and almost ran to her room. What was he doing? He'd said they would grow old and remember this year. Did he mean grow old together? She'd told him unequivocally that wasn't going to happen, but when he talked, his words made sense. He'd been through real pain in his life, while she got hung up on one silly Christmas, but he still made time to comfort her and didn't belittle her. She scrambled out of her clothes and pulled on the only evening dress she had with her, a red satin mini that sat off her shoulders and hugged her figure before flaring into a wider skirt.

Giving into Farid was the easy short-term solution. She picked up her phone and spotted a message from her sister.

ALICE: Just touching base. What are you getting Ma and Dad for Christmas? I never know what to buy them. Was talking to them earlier. Dad says you've been having trouble with a refugee who's trying to marry you. What's going on? I know Dad's stupidly paranoid, but seriously? Where has he got that idea?

Holly slowly closed her eyes and breathed. Her father would never understand how much Farid meant to her. Maybe she'd underestimated it herself.

CHAPTER TWENTY-THREE

Farid

A princess in a movie couldn't have looked better. Holly was more dazzling than a ruby under a spotlight. She was beautiful in her pyjamas, in her lounge clothes, in the elf costume, in nothing, but this was a whole new level.

'Holly, you are so beautiful.' Farid took both her hands in his own and kissed the backs of them.

'You look damn good yourself.'

'We will be quite the pair, no?'

'Come on then.' She smiled, but the sad eyes he'd spotted the first time he saw her were back. Since those early days, her pale-blue irises had sparkled. He was sure he'd succeeded in bringing magic into her life. But she'd shut the door. She didn't want what he had to give and he'd run out of tricks – almost. Could he accept her conditions? Accept she was leaving and their time would end? Yes. But it would cleave his heart in two. He'd already told her he would do anything for her. If that was the task, then he would follow through.

One last roll of the dice remained. Before the night was out, he'd try it.

Holly lifted her jacket from the hook in the hall and passed Farid his. This house had been as much a home for him as his own side of the cottage. The companionship with Holly had given him so much joy in a new and unfamiliar place. It had made it more bearable and transformed the life he'd been forced to accept into something he'd happily have chosen. Could he trust the universe to send him someone else as perfect as her after she'd gone? Maybe he wouldn't have to.

He smiled at her as he pulled on his jacket. 'When I say you are beautiful, *jamilati,* I don't just mean your face, your hair, your body, your clothes, I mean everything inside too. You're fun, you work hard, you have spirit, passion and when it gets mixed together, it makes a beautiful Holly.'

'Farid, you missed a vocation in life. You should be some kind of salesman, you can charm anyone.'

He took her hand. 'I only speak the truth.'

She squeezed his fingers and they left.

'I'll drive, *jamilati,* then you can drink.'

'Thank you. And, Farid, I'm sorry. What I just told you sounds so petty compared to what you've had to deal with this past year.'

'It's ok. My biggest hurt is not having my family. Your biggest hurt was losing the man you set your heart on. Both are pains caused by love.'

'Exactly.' The look in her eyes reminded him *this is a short-term thing.*

His chest ached like someone had dropped a life-sized stone Santa on him. *Must concentrate.* These roads in the dark were awful. Holly sat quietly and he mirrored her. He drove across the island to the east side and into the driveway of the Glen Lodge Hotel.

Inside the foyer, soft music played, and people milled around.

'Nice place.' Holly pushed open the left side of a double swing door into a twinkling main room. A wooden dance floor gleamed in the centre. 'There's Robyn.' Holly waved to her. A man close to her caught Farid's eye. Per Hansen, looking better groomed than usual in a smart shirt and tie, though his flyaway grey curls were as unruly as ever.

'Hi,' Robyn said. 'How are you?'

'Good,' Holly said. 'I've sent you an email.'

'I got it, thanks. I'm happy for you to work anywhere. I didn't realise you were leaving so soon after Christmas but it makes no difference to me. Most of my work is done remotely anyway.'

'Great.'

The knife in Farid's chest twisted a little more. Holly was making plans and they didn't involve him. How could he prove he wasn't the same as Gavin? Whoever he was, he'd cut her deep. And missed out. Why would anyone turn down the chance of a wonderful life with the beautiful Holly?

'Hello.' A hand clapped Farid on the shoulder.

'Hi, Per. How are you?'

'Very good. I have my whole family here, so I couldn't be happier.'

Farid easily picked out Per's three sons; they were tall, handsome and had blond curls of various lengths.

'Magnus is our eldest.' Per pointed to the tallest son, who had his arm around a smiling woman. 'He's here with his wife, Taylor. And that's Jakob with his wife, Livvi, and our two grandchildren.' Jakob had a little princess on his hip, chatting and pointing at the lights. His wife had a large baby sleeping on her shoulder, and she talked to Per's wife. 'And Carl, of course, you met him at the carol service.'

'Ah, yes.' Robyn's husband. Robyn and Holly were still chatting about business. With her diverted and all the family scenes surrounding him, the shard of loneliness in his soul pricked. He had none of this. Take away Holly and he was just Farid. Single. Alone.

Tables were set around the edge of the dance floor with mini fibre-optic Christmas trees, glowing alternate colours that slowly faded out, then reappeared. Georgia waved to them from a busy table close to the window. 'We've got seats for you here.'

Farid pulled out the chair for Holly to sit first. He nodded at Archie. Another couple sat next to him. There was Autumn from The Boat Shack, cradling her tummy. A tall, dark-haired man stroked her back. Beside him was Blair with his partner,

Rebekah. A woman possibly in her late forties was next to her and, on her other side, Mike.

'Hello, Mike.'

'Hi, Farid. How are you?'

'Good, thank you.'

'This is Vicky, my wife-to-be.'

Farid nodded to her.

'And my son, Blair, and Rebekah.'

'We met before. Hi.'

'Autumn is Vicky's daughter,' Mike said. 'And Richard is her husband.'

'Hi,' the dark-haired man said.

'And this is Farid,' Georgia said. 'For those who don't know. He's working on the estate with us, and this is Holly, my old uni pal, though just to warn you, none of you need to know details of the stuff we got up to.'

'Even me?' Archie said.

'Especially you.' Georgia leaned on him and he patted her back. 'So glad you two could make it.' Georgia looked between Farid and Holly. 'And it's so cute you're together.'

'Yes,' Holly said quietly. 'I'll get drinks.'

'Let me,' Archie said. 'I'll get it. What would you both like?'

'White wine, please,' Holly said. 'And thanks.'

'Irn Bru for me, please,' Farid said.

Archie headed for the bar and they chatted among themselves. Georgia and Autumn were talented at telling stories that kept everyone smiling.

'I actually did fall for Richard on a trip here,' Autumn said.

'As in, you tripped and fell down a hill,' Blair chipped in.

Autumn covered her face and chuckled. 'Yes.'

'I still don't know how you didn't break your neck,' Richard said.

Farid's eyes strayed to Holly. She was resolutely silent, barely even smiling when the others laughed. As soon as she had a drink in hand, she knocked it back.

A microphone crackled into action and a thin woman with spiky white hair tapped it. 'Thank you for coming, everyone. We have quite a night lined up for you; some of our most talented islanders will entertain you.'

Georgia patted Archie on the knee. Farid didn't have to wait long to discover why. The woman at the microphone called Archie's name and he took a seat behind a grand piano in the corner. Soon, beautiful music filled the room. Farid still wasn't sure of the names of the songs but he could tell they were Christmassy. Georgia beamed at her husband. Holly half-rolled her eyes, her gaze landing on Farid. For a few moments, he stared deep into her pale-blue irises and his heart wept. She had the power of love but chose to withhold it. He'd tried everything to help her unleash it. He had very little left. Only his last resort. He stretched out his hand and lifted hers from her lap. The music swept around the room and Farid caressed her fingers in his, only releasing them to applaud Archie.

He stayed seated at the piano. The woman with the short spiky hair announced, 'Thank you, Archie. Now, Magnus and Taylor Hansen, if you'll take the stage, please.'

Per's eldest son and his smiling young wife climbed the steps onto a small stage area behind two microphones. The onlookers hushed and the duo sang a hauntingly beautiful version of 'Silent Night'. Farid took Holly's hand again as the crystal-clear notes echoed around. His chest filled and a lump rose in his throat. Visions of home, family, and Holly flooded his mind. He wiped a tear from under his eye with his palm as the song finished.

After a couple more, Archie and the singers returned to their tables. A band of youngsters got up and struck up some jaunty music, inviting people to dance.

'Do you fancy this?' Holly said. 'Proper Scottish dancing. Your first ceilidh.'

'I don't know how.'

'Me neither but most people make it up as they go along.'

'Then how can I refuse?'

Holly led him to the floor and they tried to copy the people around them. Her smile returned as Farid twirled her and they almost collapsed, laughing. 'We'll get removed.' Her eyes watered and she clasped her hand at her chest. The tune ended and every-one clapped. 'I need air. Come over here, the window's open.'

She stood beside it, half-hidden behind the giant Christmas tree and fanned her face.

Farid took hold of her shoulders and drew her into him, kissing her firmly on the lips. She clutched his cheeks and returned it.

'We've had our moments, haven't we?' she said as they broke apart, resting their foreheads together.

He held her close. '*Bahebek, jamilati.*'

'What does that mean, Farid? I know it isn't Merry Christmas.'

'I love you.'

'What?' She pulled back and stared at him.

'Please. I'm sorry if that's not what you wanted to hear, but that's how I feel. That's how I've felt for a long time.'

'That's what you've been saying to me?'

'Yes. And why not? I love you, Holly. Why is it so bad an idea that we stay here together? Wouldn't you stay? We could try – see what it's like, even for a little while. This could be our home, together.'

She shook her head and backed away. 'No, Farid. No.' Her hands rose in front of her like a shield. 'I told you already. That isn't the life I want. I can't.'

'Why not? You wanted it before.'

'I thought I did. But maybe that just showed me how stupid I was to want that. I've had so much more success in my life since letting go of all that.'

'You succeed in life because you have skill, not because you gave up on love.'

'What you feel isn't love, it's lust.'

'Not true, Holly. I know the difference. I might not have the experience but I have a heart.'

'I'm sorry, Farid. Now, please... I need to go to the bathroom.'

He watched her skim the edge of the dance floor on the side of the bar, avoiding where Georgia was at the table with her friends.

He ran his hands over his hair. What now? Go after her? Leave her alone? He'd played his last card and she ripped it into a hundred pieces. Lust? No. She was wrong. This was a lot more. His previous relationships might be non-existent but he was in touch with his own heart and knew his own feelings a lot better than her. The lights on the Christmas tree twinkled beside him, mocking his misplaced faith in himself, love and Holly.

CHAPTER TWENTY-FOUR

Holly

Holly stared at her reflection in the mirror in the toilets. She couldn't hide in here all night. At some point, she'd have to face the music... or at least Farid. What he wanted was impossible. And love! It was laughable. He couldn't possibly understand love. She'd had enough relationships over the years to know love didn't exist. Or if it did, it didn't last.

Lust existed. Companionship existed. Occasionally, the two overlapped for a while and gave the illusion of love. Her mind flew to Georgia and Archie, to Robyn and Carl and to the families she'd met at Santa's grotto. Love existed for them, didn't it? She braced herself on the tiled counter surrounding the large oval sinks. Bile rose. Oh no, was she going to throw up? Other people found love, she didn't. Because love meant compromise. At twenty-six she'd been willing to sacrifice everything for Gavin but he wasn't ready. Now she was thirty-two and a twenty-six-year-old was suggesting she took a chance on him. Could she?

Farid had the car. She had to go back with him but what would they talk about now? This was worse than Gavin-gate. She'd left that Christmas meal humiliated. Did Farid feel like that now? Had she just done the same thing to him? At least no one had overheard. She'd suffered the humiliation in front of the Sinclairs. But would everyone be asking questions? How would Farid reply?

Holly left the toilets and sidled into the main room, scanning around. Farid wasn't at the table with Georgia. She was laughing with Archie and their friends. People were dancing to a different band and Magnus and Taylor Hansen were singing again. There was Farid standing at another table. His work colleague, Per Hansen, had his arm over Farid's shoulder and seemed to be explaining something. Farid nodded and smiled along, but Holly knew him too well now; he wasn't really listening. His mind was elsewhere.

Taking a long, deep breath, she approached. He saw her from well off but couldn't move because of Per.

'Hi,' Holly said, and Per grinned.

'Ah, here's your lovely lady.' He released Farid. 'I'll let the two of you catch up on your dancing and see you on Monday. It's Christmas Eve, so we'll clock off early.'

'Thanks, and Merry Christmas to your family.'

Per clapped him on the back, leaving him to stare at Holly.

'Can we go, please? I'm sorry to spoil the party.' She looked at her feet.

'Of course, let's go.'

They collected their belongings from the table. Georgia stood to wish them a Merry Christmas and kissed Holly on both cheeks, whispering, 'have a nice night,' as she reached the second side.

Could Georgia have grabbed a more wrong end of the proverbial stick? Holly wasn't going home for a night of passion with Farid. She was heading back to see if she could get a ferry off the island the following day and find somewhere else to hide for Christmas – maybe forever.

The silence of the journey home was absolute. The pitch black of the bleak mid-winter closed in around them like a noxious gas, suffocating them.

'Holly,' Farid said quietly as they approached the gates of Ardnish. 'I didn't mean to offend you, not in any way. I'm sorry my feelings are so awful for you to hear.'

'They're not awful. They just aren't true.'

'How can you say that? You don't rule my heart.' His tone was heated. 'I know how I feel. You just don't want to hear it.'

'Is that what you think?' Adrenaline spiked, blocking any chance of his words making sense but ensuring they battered every nerve. 'What we had was good. Very good, and I'm not denying it. But it was lust, nothing more. I understand your position. You're lonely. You want a way out. But it's not me.'

'That's not what I'm doing.'

'What?'

'Trying to force you into a relationship so I can stay here. If that's what you think, then you don't know me at all. Never would I behave like that. The love I have for you is deep within and has nothing to do with where you live, what your country is, or anything like that. It comes from the feeling my soul has when it's next to yours. On its own, it's a half-life but with you, it's complete.'

Holly held her hand to her mouth and stared into the blackness. Do not cry. His words cut so deep. They penetrated her half of the soul. But it was a dream, not reality. 'One day you'll find your true love. And then you'll know it wasn't me.'

'Keep telling yourself that,' he said, then muttered something in Arabic.

When they rolled up at the cottage, Holly turned to him; her hand shook as she fought to control it. The pain in her chest doubled. 'Well... Bye.'

'Goodbye, *jamilati.*' He stared forward.

She unclipped her seatbelt and eased out the door.

'*Ana Bahebek,*' he said as she closed it.

She ran up the path and into the house. Not even bothering with the light, she pulled off her coat and used the torch on her phone to get into her room. Throwing off her dress and shoes, she climbed under the bedcovers and trembled. She had to find the strength to get through this. She would and she could get over him. Holly Devaney was best on her own and she didn't need a man to make her happy. No way. Why then couldn't she convince her aching soul that was true?

CHAPTER TWENTY-FIVE

Farid

Sunday dragged on forever. Holly was just through the wall but the cottage was silent. Maybe she'd gone out or left. It wasn't Farid's business to know or care, but he did. Every twenty minutes or so, he would look out the window either front or back, hoping for a sight or sound of her, knowing it would change nothing. His soul ached for its mate.

He tried television, music, and reading, but nothing kept his attention. Monday morning couldn't come quick enough. The significance of Christmas Eve was lost on him; it was just another day in the office – or in his case, the forest.

Mike had finished up on Friday, but Per showed up in a Santa hat with a wrapped box. 'Merry Christmas.' He handed it to Farid.

'Thank you so much. I'm sorry, I have nothing in return.'

'That's quite all right. We get enough as it is. You enjoy it. If we get this cleared up, we'll leave as soon as. I want to spend the day waiting for Santa with Polly and Rory. There's nothing so magical as seeing it through the eyes of the children.'

'I can do this myself,' Farid said. 'You go back to your family.'

'Oh, that's very kind. But don't you want to get away and spend some time with your lovely girlfriend?'

'Holly's working. I will do this. It's my gift to you.'

'Thank you, son. You're a kind lad.' Per clapped Farid's shoulder. 'I forgot Holly was working. She's gone to visit Robyn this morning, hasn't she? Carl said so.'

'Did he?' Farid gave a little cough, hoping to hide his ignorance, but it meant Holly was still on the island.

'Yes. He drove me over this morning. He's doing something for Georgia. If you're sure about doing this, I'll nip to Monarch's Lodge and see how he's getting on. And I can fill Archie in on what we've got left to do.'

'Yes, no problem.'

'I hope your first Christmas in Scotland is one to remember.'

'Thank you and Merry Christmas to you too.' He'd remember this Christmas forever, though not for the right reasons.

He rolled up the sleeves of the red tartan lumberjack shirt and started throwing cut logs onto the pile. Per had meant only to clear the section they'd been working on but what was the rush and where else was there to go? Farid carried on, clearing the undergrowth and making way for the area they would tackle in the new year. A year Farid had hoped would bring something good. Now it looked as bleak and grim as the last.

Why had he let himself go with Holly? What had seemed like a harmless mission was now a blight on his ever-growing list of misjudgements.

If he'd kept his mouth shut and his head down two years ago, he might not be here at all. He and his family may eventually have been forced to flee but who knew? Maybe following his convictions had led him into more trouble than it was worth. Now, he'd done the same in his personal life. This time, no one would have to deal with the fallout but himself. His attempts to assimilate had backfired. So much for learning about the magic of Christmas. This was just another day in the cold, worse than the others because it was lonely. Everyone else was home with their families.

'Why?' He glanced heavenward. Why had he behaved like a fool? He'd escaped the danger at home but he couldn't protect himself from himself. His family would be horrified at what he'd done, laid himself bare at the feet of a woman, let her use him, then cast him out. Maybe she was right. He'd been infatuated. Now he was alone.

His chest ached. Would he ever escape and be free? No matter what he did, he couldn't win. 'For Farid, there is no home, no joy, no love.' He slung aside a pile of branches, letting them clatter to the ground.

The work built up a sweat on his brow and he stopped to catch his breath. This self-deprecation wasn't him. He was a survivor. He could get through this.

A twig snapped on the path behind. His heart skipped. Had Holly come to find him? A man's voice called out, 'Dexter, get back here.' A liver-coloured pointer came bounding through the undergrowth.

'Hey.'

The dog loped up to him, wagging its narrow tail.

'Dexter!' the man shouted. It was Archie. He stepped off the path and a second pointer stood at his side, poised and calm. 'Oh, hello, Farid. I wondered why he ran off. Come here, Dexter.' The dog dropped his nose and sniffed a bush.

'He's not as well-behaved as this one.' Farid pointed to the dog at Archie's side.

'No, this is Duchess. She's his mother and she has more decorum. I thought you'd gone home.'

The word sliced into Farid. Home? Did he have a true home? 'No, not yet.'

'Per called by and said you were getting on great. I'm happy to keep you on in the new year, but there's not enough work here to last indefinitely.'

'Yeah, for sure. I should look for other things.' Of course this couldn't last.

'There will be lots of other jobs on the estate.' Archie gave a little smile; his expression was warm. 'I'm not kicking you out. You can have the cottage as long as you need it, no strings attached. I don't want you to feel used and abused. Khalif told me you were talented at your job and I'd like to help you get back to that. If that's something you'd like.'

'I would, but my qualification is not accepted here and I don't have a computer.'

Archie rubbed his chin. 'I didn't think about that. I have a laptop at the house you could have just now. Maybe not the most up to date but you're welcome to it. I wish I'd considered that sooner.'

'You've already done enough.'

'Hardly. Nothing I've done has been any trouble. Why don't you call in later and I'll give you the laptop?'

'It's very generous.'

'Consider it a Christmas gift. Georgia will probably want to wrap it up in bows and strings and use half a roll of tape in the process.'

Farid smiled. 'She is very lovely.'

'Yes, she is. And I'm very lucky. We only met two Christmases ago. Best Christmas ever.' Archie's eyes lost focus for a few seconds and he seemed to watch something play out in his mind.

'I'll come round later. Thank you.'

'No problem.' Archie clapped him on the shoulder. 'And go home, give yourself a break. You deserve it.'

Go home? To face a cold empty house?

Chapter Twenty-Six

Holly

Holly's plans to evade Christmas were often crazy but this had to be the craziest ever. Working on Christmas Eve was just the beginning. Talking in person to Robyn was unnecessary but it would pass the time more enjoyably than being alone. As soon as she pulled up at the beautiful cottage in Carsaig, she spotted the first flaw. Robyn wasn't likely to want to spend Christmas Eve talking shop. She had a husband and would want to spend the time with him doing whatever couples normally did on Christmas Eve.

So her visit would have to be shorter than planned. After, she'd drive around the island, stop wherever, and maybe take photos. But not return until well after dark. This she would repeat for the next two days and she'd leave on the twenty-seventh, by that time people's Christmases would be over and she could find a hotel to crash in for a day or two while she sorted where to live next.

Robyn welcomed her and they sat in her living room on the grey sofas, sipping hot chocolates. The room was a cross between the Ikea catalogue and a Nordic retreat. Holly huddled into the corner of the sofa where a big furry blanket covered the arm. Like snuggling on the rug in front of the fire with Farid. Oh, to be there now, with his arms around her and his voice whispering to her. Best Christmas gift ever. But love like his was for life and not just Christmas. She couldn't guarantee her restless feet would stick around long enough not to break him again in another few months, weeks or even days. She'd made her bed.

Beside Robyn, curled up on the sofa, was a cute little dog. Robyn stroked her as she checked the information on her tablet.

'So, if we have a section here where clients can click directly to the files.' Robyn stopped talking and rubbed her lower tummy.

'Are you ok?'

Robyn had done that on another occasion, but this time her face was twisted. 'I might need to go to the hospital.'

'Why?' Holly leaned forward.

'We haven't told anyone but I'm pregnant.'

'And is something wrong?'

'I had an ectopic pregnancy three years ago. I had to have one of my tubes removed. It's never been guaranteed that I could have kids and now... Oh, god. It might be happening again. This was how it started before.'

'Oh, god.' Holly stood up. 'Where's Carl?'

'He's driven up to Ardnish; he had something to do. I suspect it's a surprise Christmas present he's been hiding there from me.'

'Come on then, I'll take you to the hospital. You can call him on the way and he can meet us there.'

'Ok, thank you. I hope it isn't another ectopic. If it is, then that's it. I won't ever have kids.'

'Let's get it checked. It might be ok.' Her heartbeat stuttered. 'I've never been pregnant, but my sister has two kids and she had lots of twinges and pains with both of them. So, let's keep hoping.' She kept talking as they made their way to the car, more to keep herself calm than Robyn. Her gut told her this wouldn't end well. Poor Robyn. The little dog followed and Holly lifted her. 'Do you want me to put her in the house?'

'Can she come?'

'Sure.' Holly placed her on Robyn's knee and Robyn held her like a hot water bottle on her lap. The road from Carsaig was narrow and twisty. Holly had a prickle of panic at every bend, not in case of meeting other cars but that any sudden movement would hurt Robyn. It was like driving with a glass of water on the bonnet and trying not to spill it.

Robyn got out her phone but the reception wasn't good enough to make a call. 'I should have called before we left.'

'We might get 4G further up.' The island loomed around, so much bigger than she'd thought. Mountains towered alongside them as they wound through the glen. Beautiful waterfalls cascaded down the rocky hillsides and low clouds gathered above them.

Craignure, the village where the ferry docked, was also home to the hospital. So far to go in a hurry. Robyn attempted a call again and finally got a connection as they motored through the tiny seaside village of Lochdon.

'We're only five minutes away,' Robyn said. 'I've been trying to get a signal the whole way.'

Carl's voice rattled faintly. What was he saying? Robyn ended the call and gripped her phone. 'He's at his mum's house. Ten minutes and he'll be here.'

'Ok, that's good.' Holly's brain functions were now limited to getting Robyn into the hospital. The car park was busy, and Holly groaned as she circled it. 'Please, let there be a space.'

'There's an overflow car park.'

'Let's hope there's room in there.' Surely she wasn't going to be stuck with a pregnant woman on Christmas Eve with no room in the car park. Lots of free spaces presented themselves in the overflow and Holly slammed into the first one. 'Right, let's get you in. If I wind down the windows, we can leave your dog here.'

'Florrie's her name.'

'Sweet. I fancy a dog but my lifestyle doesn't suit it.'

'I used to be like that. But once I tried, I never looked back. I realised life isn't static. Changing things doesn't have to hurt. I just hope I can make the next step.' She rubbed her tummy. 'I can't bear going through that again.'

'Come on, let's get inside. The sooner they check it, the better.'

Holly dallied alongside Robyn, eyeing her in case she collapsed or shattered. As Robyn explained the problem to the triage nurse,

Holly backed off. Where was Carl? She didn't mind waiting but this was a job for Robyn's husband.

The nurse sent them to the waiting area.

'They're going to do a scan straightaway.'

'That's good.' Holly rested her head on the wall behind the soft seats. Music played from a tiny TV screen. 'Do You Hear What I Hear?' What did she hear? When she closed her eyes, all she could hear was Farid's voice. Exactly what she wanted to hear right now. He always knew what to say to make her feel better.

'Why are you leaving?' Robyn asked.

'You know.' Holly opened her eyes and shrugged.

'Not really. I thought you and Farid were together, but he's not leaving, is he?'

'No, he's not and we're not together.'

'Oh. You seemed so happy together. I was sure…' She stopped and looked up. 'Carl!' Getting to her feet, she embraced the curly-haired bear of a man. He held her close, rubbing his hand down her back.

Holly curled into herself as he quizzed Robyn. Before she'd answered all his questions, they were called.

'If I have to go to the mainland or anything, can you look after Florrie?' Robyn asked Holly. 'Carl's mum will take her if you can get her there.'

'No problem. You go and see what they say.'

Holly closed her eyes and leaned back again. Farid's voice whispered in her imagination. '*Bahebek, jamiliti.*' All those times he'd been saying, 'I love you.' Not love. She shook her head. It couldn't be love. Why not? What had Robyn said about life not being static? *Have I got set in my ways?* Was there harm in trying something different? If being with Farid brought her so much joy, why wasn't she embracing it? Hanging about here wouldn't be any harder than looking for a new place every few weeks. Maybe there was joy in stopping and being still. And how much more enjoyable would it be with Farid at her side?

Her heart squirmed when she opened her eyes and remembered where she was. What was happening to Robyn? Holly wasn't religious but she pressed her hands together. 'Please, god, universe, anyone, please let Robyn be ok. Please let the baby be ok.'

The door Robyn and Carl had gone through opened and closed several times. People went in and out. Holly watched it. Even when she was focused elsewhere, she had it in her peripheral vision, waiting. Waiting for the moment when—

The door swung open and they stepped out. Holly's chest caved. Carl was supporting Robyn and her eyes were puffy and red. She held her hand to her lips. Holly wanted to vanish into the floor, not to be a spectator to their private grief. What would happen now? Would they airlift Robyn to the mainland and have an operation that wouldn't just ruin her Christmas, but her chances of ever becoming a mum?

Holly got to her feet. 'Hey.' She kept her gaze low.

'Oh god.' Robyn's fingers slid away from her lips and she blinked away tears.

'I'm sorry.' A lump swelled in Holly's throat.

'It's twins,' Robyn said. 'And they're both fine. It's all fine, just growing pains.' Tears streamed down her face and Carl laughed through his own as he hugged her.

'What?' Holly found herself wiping her eyes. 'Oh, thank god. And twins? No way.'

'I know. It's unbelievable.'

'Wait until I tell Mum,' Carl said.

'And Magnus.' Robyn chuckled.

'Oh, hell, yes.' Carl smiled at Holly. 'Magnus married a twin and got caught up in one of the most bizarre twin swaps ever.'

Holly beamed between the two of them. 'Well, these two appear to be troublemakers already.' She eyed Robyn's tummy. 'Now, are you both ok?'

'Never been better,' Carl said.

'Excellent,' Holly said. 'I've got your dog in the car, so let's get her back to the two of you.'

'Thank you so much,' Robyn said.

'I would say anytime, but I'm hoping it doesn't happen again.'

'I agree,' Carl said. 'But thanks a million. You better get back. Dad said he sent Farid home early so you guys could enjoy Christmas Eve together and here's us stealing it from you.'

Holly didn't reply but something seismic had shifted in her rock-hard, unrelenting heart. Farid had started the quake but now the walls were crumbling. Once her heart was free, it would lead her straight back to his arms. The only problem was, would he have her? She'd been such a crazy bitch, he'd have every right to send her packing. Somehow she'd make it worth his while.

Chapter Twenty-Seven

Farid

Chilled air stung Farid as he finished clearing the logs. He thrust his hands into his pockets and tramped back to the pickup. Georgia and Archie were generous and he was ready to accept their gift. A laptop would help. Holly did everything remotely; could he do something similar?

Georgia answered the door like she'd been standing behind it waiting for him to knock. 'Come in.' Her beautiful smile split her face.

'Hi.' Farid ruffed up his hair. 'I don't want to interrupt your Christmas Eve, but Archie said—'

'You're not interrupting. Archie told me. He's nipped up to the office at the main house to get the cables for the laptop.'

'Ah, ok.'

'Come and sit down. Would you like a drink? I could do a hot chocolate with all the trimmings. I need one myself.'

'Ok, sure. Thank you.'

Farid made his way into the bright lounge area. The mantelpiece had very Georgia-esque décor around it. He recognised her handiwork in the greenery and the lighting, so similar to Holly's cottage.

'You won't believe the afternoon I've had.' Georgia placed a mug on the coffee table in front of Farid and slumped onto the opposite sofa with her own. 'I've just had Carl on the phone. Apparently, Robyn had to go to the hospital earlier.'

'Oh? Is she ok?'

'She is now. She's pregnant.' Georgia shook her head and grinned.

'Wow.'

'Holly was with her this morning and Robyn felt some twinges and thought something was wrong. Holly took her to the hospital and, when they ran the scan, they discovered it was twins.'

'Double wow.'

'Carl sounded so happy. It's sweet. He was my first friend when I arrived here. It makes me all emotional.' She fanned her face and blinked. 'I love the way it's worked out.'

'Sounds great.' He sipped his hot drink, savouring the warmth of the cup and brushing a fleck of cream from the tip of his nose. Everyone's Christmas dreams were coming true. Farid's mind lingered on what Georgia had said about Holly. She was still here and that surely meant she'd be here for Christmas. She might catch the last boat today but none sailed on Christmas Day or Boxing Day.

'So, are you and Holly spending the day together tomorrow?' Georgia asked.

Farid stared into his mug, swirling the remaining cream into the dark depths of the chocolate. 'No. We're not together.'

'What?'

'It was just a fling.'

'No way. The two of you were getting on so well.'

'We were, but Holly... Pah.' He gulped some more hot chocolate, burning the back of his throat. 'She is stubborn. She doesn't want to be long-term with someone. So, she's leaving. I crossed all the lines and acted like a stupid man.'

'What do you mean?'

'I told her how I felt. I said I loved her.'

Georgia tilted her head and her eyebrows raised in the middle. 'That is so lovely.'

'She didn't think so.'

'I bet she does really.'

'No, she doesn't. She hates Christmas and she hates relationships because of some man.'

'Gavin?'

'You know him?'

'A little. They dated at uni and they were together for a few years. I was sure they'd get married. Holly always wanted the big white wedding but now she seems to have gone completely the other way.'

'Was he a bad man?'

'Not at all. He was a bit dull, but not bad. When Holly split with him, she didn't see anyone else – not in the long term. She moved about and I couldn't keep track of where she was living or who she was seeing. I don't know why they split though.'

'She told me why. It's not for me to tell you. But I'm not him. Just because he didn't truly love her doesn't mean I won't.'

'I know that, but you're right, she's stubborn. I wish I could help, but I suspect if I get involved, she'll get annoyed with me.'

'It's too late.' Farid sighed.

A scuffling in the hall alerted them to Archie's return. The two dogs hustled into the room, panting. One of them jumped on Farid, wagging his tail.

'Dexter,' Georgia said. 'Honestly, that dog is named after a serial killer and sometimes he's just about as insane.'

'He is not named after a serial killer,' Archie said.

The dog licked Farid's face and he scrunched up his nose, trying to ward off the giant tongue.

'Dexter, get down.' The dog jumped down. 'Into your room, both of you.' Archie held the door and pointed; both dogs skulked out. He patted their heads as they passed. 'That's it, go and chill.'

'They don't listen to me,' Georgia said.

'Dexter doesn't listen to anyone,' Archie said. 'Now, Farid, I've got the cables and done a reset on this laptop. Hopefully, it'll be ok.'

'That is so kind, truly.'

'No problem.' Archie handed it over, then sat beside Georgia.

'Tomorrow,' she said, 'You can come here for Christmas lunch. I don't want you sitting up there alone.'

'No. I don't want to get in the way.'

'You won't be in the way,' Archie said. 'Christmas is for families and you're part of the Ardnish family.'

'Exactly,' Georgia said.

'That's kind,' Farid said. 'But what about Holly?'

'She can come too,' Archie said.

'That's the problem.'

Archie furrowed his brow.

'Things aren't going too well,' Georgia said.

'It's Christmas Eve,' Archie said. 'That's when the magic happens.'

Georgia beamed. 'It did for us.'

What did she mean?

Farid's scepticism must have shown because she continued, 'Two years ago, things looked bad for us, but on Christmas Eve, Archie proposed.'

'After you surprised me by decorating this house.' They smiled at each other and the depth of love in their eyes was overwhelming. Exactly how Farid felt when he looked at Holly. No way was this just lust.

'Don't give up,' Georgia said. 'Talk to her. One more try. The last push.'

'She's left the island,' Farid said. 'She said she was going to.'

Georgia frowned. 'Would she visit Robyn if she was leaving?'

'Maybe.'

'I think she's still here.'

Farid wasn't so sure. He'd used up all his tries already and his body was spent. When he got back, darkness was closing in around the cottage in the late afternoon. Holly's car wasn't there. Had she caught the last boat and sailed away? Or perhaps she'd arranged to stay with Robyn. Maybe she was eating out. Alone? Why couldn't she have yielded? They could be inside together, snuggling on the sofa, watching movies, cuddling, eating, drinking, kissing, and enjoying this first Christmas Eve in Scotland.

Instead, Farid went into the house, pulled on a pair of pyjamas and lay on his sofa. And so this was Christmas?

Chapter Twenty-Eight

The happy tears Holly had shed with Robyn and Carl earlier wouldn't be forgotten quickly. She drove towards Tobermory, still smiling. And to hell with it, she was having music on, even if the first thing that belted out was bloody Mariah Carey and 'All I Want for Christmas Is You'. Well, damn it, all she wanted for Christmas was Farid. She couldn't bear the idea of never seeing him again.

But she'd blown it. *What a frigging idiot.* She'd been so vehement in her aversion to relationships she'd cast him off. Even now the idea terrified her, but after going less than twenty-four hours without him, the thought of giving him up terrified her more. She was like a puppy wrenched from its basket and left out in the snow. Who would give her the cuddles she needed to get her back where she wanted to be?

Gavin had shattered her dreams six years ago, making her question what she'd grown up wishing for. But maybe it hadn't been just the man who wasn't right, maybe the time hadn't been right either. What about now?

She whizzed the car into the car park in Tobermory and checked her phone. 'Oops.' Several missed calls had registered. Her parents, Alice, and Georgia. Who to return first...? Or leave them all? No one had left a message, so it was unlikely any of them were urgent. In that case, Georgia's seemed the most pressing. She was on the island, after all, and she might want something picked up. Holly's parents and Alice were more likely to be doing the *I can't believe you're missing another Christmas with us* speech.

'Hi, Georgia, did you call?' Holly zapped the car shut and nipped towards the main street. Fairy lights glittered in the shop windows like something from a film.

'Hi, I just wanted to check you were ok after the hospital trip today. Carl rang; they're so happy. Thank goodness you were there.'

'Yeah. I'm glad it's worked out for them.'

'Farid was here.'

'Was he?' As Georgia's nosiness was legendary, Holly knew exactly why she was bringing it up.

'I said I wouldn't interfere but...'

'You're going to anyway?'

'Yup,' Georgia said. 'I'll say my piece and be done.'

'Fine, let me have it.'

'Farid isn't Gavin. I don't know what happened with Gavin but I can guess it wasn't pleasant. Whatever it was, Farid doesn't deserve to be tarred with the same brush. He's a good guy and all it seems he's done wrong is tell the truth about how he feels. Would it be so hard to give him a chance?'

Holly gazed into a gift shop window and the icy Christmas display twinkled back. 'I agree with you. I've been stupid. How can I put it right? I don't know what to say. I made an idiot of myself – exactly what I did with Gavin and he couldn't forgive me for it.'

'Farid will, Holly. No matter what you've done, he'll forgive you. Now, for heaven's sake, go and see him.'

'Ok, I will, but I'm in Tobermory. I need to get some things.'

'Just don't leave it too late.'

They wished each other Merry Christmas and Holly ended the call. She could do this. First, she had to check in with her family. Number one, Alice.

ME: Hi. Hope you have a great Christmas. Sorry for disappearing off radar. Christmas has been pretty crap for me since 'Gavin-gate'. And before you start bad-mouthing him, I should fess up. He didn't propose to me out of the blue and hurt my feelings. It was the other way round. I proposed to him and made an arse of myself. Eeek. Guess I should have owned it from the start. Anyway, enjoy Christmas and I'll see you in the new year. XX

Right. Done. She exhaled slowly. Now, Ma and Dad. As she scrolled through her contacts, a message head popped up. She frowned at the little picture. Speak of the devil. Gavin. What was he messaging her about? Surely nothing could go wrong on

Christmas Eve? Was that her fate for Christmas Day? To spend it virtually with him, trying to debug a programme?

GAVIN SINCLAIR: Holly, I feel I need to send this message and not let another Christmas go by without acknowledging it. I'm sorry it's taken me so long. When you proposed to me, I got the shock of my life. We were only twenty-six and, in my mind, I hadn't thought we were anywhere near marrying or even getting engaged. Now, I'm thirty-two and I realise I was naïve, narrow-minded, and selfish. I've never come close to meeting anyone else who was as special as you. I know our time has passed and I won't insult you or your intelligence by suggesting we get back together. But if I'd had my wits about me six years ago, I would have said yes. The solid friendship we built our relationship on could easily have grown into a robust marriage over the years. I was afraid to commit so young, afraid of what it might mean in the long run.

All that remains is for me to wish you well and offer up my sincerest apologies for the appalling response I gave to your Christmas surprise. Merry Christmas. Gavin.

Wow, ok. That was unexpected. Maybe he'd done the right thing. She wasn't sure his version of a robust marriage was what she'd craved. She appreciated the message nonetheless. Her fingers whizzed over the screen.

ME: Hi. Thanks for your message. I must say I've been pretty embarrassed – understatement of the year – about it ever since. Looking back, you were right to say no. What we had was good but not spectacular, and I don't mean that cruelly; I just mean we weren't right for each other. One day I hope you find the woman who is. Merry Christmas. Holly.

Sent. Yes, she hoped he would be happy one day, just as she hoped she could after today. A few things remained. Amongst a plethora of wintery objects and trinkets in the window, one thing caught her eye and made her grin. She pushed open the door and went inside. For a small shop, it was surprisingly busy. As she waited, she made a quick call home.

Her father answered. 'Ah, you're alive.'

'Obviously. Why wouldn't I be?'

'We've been trying to reach you all day.'

'I don't always get reception. Get on messenger if you want to contact me.'

'Yes, yes,' her father said. 'We're considering it for the new year.'

'You are?' Holly pulled a face at the screen. Could they change the habit of a lifetime? Could she? Once she'd been on a path where she wanted to settle, commit to a partner, and become a family. Her humiliating attempt to secure that had knocked her off course. But Farid had pulled her back on. Now, the road was twisting back towards a future she'd thought long gone.

'We are. Now, tell us, what are you doing for Christmas Day?'

'I'm spending it with Farid.' That was what she wanted. The reality might not play out but her heart told her to say it out loud. Confessing made it real and her intentions clear.

'Hmm,' her father said. 'You're still hell-bent on seeing this man, are you?'

'Yes. He's a great guy, Dad. And one day I'd like you to meet him.'

'Well, I suppose. We should be able to trust your judgement despite the appalling fiasco with Gavin.'

'I didn't turn Gavin down. It was him who turned me down. I proposed.'

'What? Why didn't you say so before?'

'Because it was embarrassing.'

'Oh dear. And he turned you down. Silly man. Well, I know people who are very friendly with his parents and from all accounts he's a miserable so and so, so he's got what he deserved.'

Holly pressed her lips together to restrain her laugh. Her father's indignation on her behalf was funny and inflated a happy bubble in her chest.

'Maybe. But I should have considered how he felt before leaping in. It's not like that with Farid.'

'Isn't it? Are you sure?'

'Yes. I've been the opposite with him.' *Ridiculously overcautious in fact.* 'He's repeatedly told me how he feels.' And she'd dismissed it. Not only had he told her, but he'd shown her.

'Well, as long as you're sure this isn't some ploy to get into the country.'

'No, Dad. It's definitely not that.'

'I'm glad to hear it.'

That was it? No more remonstrations? He was ok with it? Was this Christmas spirit? Holly rubbed her forehead. 'Merry Christmas, Dad. Can I chat to Ma for a bit?'

'Of course, and Merry Christmas to you too.'

Holly continued to browse as she chatted to her mother and made her confession yet again. Ma was as outraged as Dad. Hopefully she wouldn't crash the Sinclair's Christmas feast to give Gavin a piece of her mind and whack him round the head with her handbag. These reactions were not what she'd expected. Gavin's rejection had made her doubt so much.

Her gaze was glued on one little object in the window. With that, Farid's festive surprise would be complete. The crowd in the shop diminished and Holly approached the till. The assistant smiled. 'How can I help you?'

'There's a little camel in the window. Can I have it, please?'

Armed with her version of the immortal camel, Holly had a quick sweep of the remaining shops. Most of them were getting ready to close early for the day but Holly found enough traditional stocking fillers to fill a bag. She grabbed the two last rolls of wrapping paper in the Co-op and a pack of tape. The Christmas Eve wrap was on.

Between Tobermory and the Ardnish estate was the village of Dervaig. On the hill above the village was a parking area with a short walk to some standing stones. She pulled into the car park. Inky blackness had descended on the island. Below, the lights of the village twinkled. She had a weird out-of-body moment as she took out the tiny camel figurine. She was one of the Magi poised on a hill above Bethlehem, surveying the town as the stars glowed overhead, seeking something... Someone. Leaning forward she looked out of her windscreen and sure enough, several bright stars sparkled like gems in the night sky. Her imagination surely, but she could have sworn one of them burned brighter than the others. Was it showing the way to a little cottage on the Ardnish estate?

She put on the car light and pulled the gifts from the bag. As soon as she took out the wrapping paper, she realised what was missing. No scissors! This could be interesting. She rummaged through her handbag. What a miracle, she had a pair of nail scissors. Cutting the paper off the roll with them was like carving a turkey with a disposable plastic knife but she did it. Slowly and steadily, the socks, chocolates, beer, wash set, puzzle book, sweets, pens and a beautiful island map rolled up in a tube were wrapped and ready. She'd bought nothing extravagant because that wasn't what Christmas was about. The festive season was, as Farid had said, about celebrating love and warmth in the coldest, darkest season of the year. Any traditions and fun they opted into along the way could be adapted and made to fit. Giving Farid a stocking full of gifts on Christmas morning was more precious than forking out on something expensive that would be forgotten in a couple of months. She didn't even have a stocking but she did have an idea.

Her heart thumped wildly as she approached the cottage at Ardnish. The track was icy but it wasn't that. How to initiate her plan? Should she go and talk to him now? Or wait until the dead of night and sneak in like Santa?

His pickup was there but his side of the cottage was in darkness. The whole building was almost invisible unless you knew it was there. Holly tapped the wheel. Was he in bed already? Surely not at six o'clock. She parked the car around the side, out of sight, killed the engine and sat in the car. What now?

CHAPTER TWENTY-NINE

Farid

With hours of nothingness ahead, Farid attempted a call home. He sat in bed surrounded by soft cushions with his phone propped on his legs. Even hearing Mama's voice would comfort him. He couldn't tell her about the pain in his soul but listening to her stories about the family would transport him into their world for a while. If the Christmas magic was real, it would spit them out of the screen and make them materialise in his house. Mama would put her arm around his back and tell him he'd been a silly boy, then hug him better. His father would tut and remind him how he'd told him about this and warned him it would happen. Nadda would scoff at the ways of Western women and Sadira would sneak up beside him and ask him to spill the gory details.

'Do you have snow?' Sadira pushed her way onto the screen.

'No, but it's icy. A man I work with told me snow is more usual in February.'

'And where is your girlfriend?'

'Sadira,' their mother said. 'Don't be so nosey.'

'Yes,' Farid said. 'Listen to Mama.'

As they chatted, he continued to navigate around the Holly questions, steering the conversation back to the family. Was that a car coming up? Switching off his camera, he jumped off the bed and padded through to the living room. He never bothered drawing the curtains; the darkness was so absolute at night.

'I'm still here, Mama. I just thought I heard something.' Keeping the light off, he squinted out the window into the pitch black. His eyes adjusted and he could make out the shape of the pickup at the end of the path, but Holly's car wasn't there. His ears were hearing the sound they wanted to hear. Whatever Georgia might think, he was sure Holly had left. He returned to his room and put his camera back on.

'Baba has something to tell you,' Mama said.

'What's that?'

'We might try to move to Scotland with you,' his father said.

'Really?' Farid said. 'You know how hard it will be?'

'Yes,' his father said. 'It means much paperwork and possibly even then it will not be accepted. I will have to prove I can work and earn enough to keep my family. None of it will be easy.'

'Then why?'

'Life is hard here too,' his father said. 'I feel we must try this. If we can reunite our family, it will be worth it.'

Farid nodded and smiled, his chest filling with a bittersweet mix of pain and hope. The likelihood of the request getting through the authorities was miniscule, especially for a man of

Khalif's age whose working life was almost over, but Farid recognised the effort on his father's part. Even if his application didn't succeed, perhaps he would be more accepting of Farid's choice. Because this was his home now. 'Thank you, Baba. I know how hard a move like that would be for you.'

'Maybe, my son, but you've shown us it can be done and the place you live looks so beautiful in all your photographs.'

'But a bit too cold,' Sadira said.

'Yes. It can be cold,' Farid said. 'But that has upsides too. Warm fires and blankets are very nice.'

'Is that what you do with your girlfriend?' Sadira giggled.

'Please, don't be so rude.' Khalif half closed his eyes. 'Whatever happens, Farid, you are a young man with your life ahead of you. What is most important is that you're happy. If being with this young woman is what that takes, then we will be fine with that. Your life has taken a different path from ours and you have to find the way that suits you.'

'Thank you, Baba.' If only the future with Holly was guaranteed. Farid had never expected a blessing from his father, yet there it was. Now, he'd have to break the news somewhere down the line that Holly wasn't his girlfriend anymore, confirming his father's suspicions about Western girls and throwing them back several degrees in his thinking. Something to worry about later. Not now.

Ending the call was a wrench and Farid stared at the ceiling, holding back tears. Everything was quiet and the icy fingers of loneliness took hold, crushing him and breaking him a little more.

His head slumped and he turned to the side, switched off the bedside lamp and let a tear fall onto his pillow.

Disorientated and a little shaky, Farid woke. His neck hurt from lying in an awkward position. A soft mattress was beneath him. He was safe. This wasn't the hostile bed of unfriendly places but the warmth and comfort of Ardnish, his island home. As his senses came around, his ears pricked at a sound. Before he could lift his head from the pillow, his heart rate picked up, pounding in his ears. He lay perfectly still, waiting for another sound. Silence. But he'd heard something. Real? Or the remnant of a dream? Someone searching for him? Friend or foe?

His brain unravelled a string of unrelated thoughts, trying to pick out something that made sense of the noise. The faint shuffling and a slight bump from the room next door. He reached for his phone and checked the time. Nine-thirty. He'd slept for a while. There it was again. He sat up. That was definitely something. It was still Christmas Eve. Would a child in this country hear the sound and believe it was Santa Claus? Was it Holly next door? His bedroom was on the outer edge of the cottage and didn't back onto her house. If she was home, he wouldn't hear her from this room.

What then? Burglars? Did people rob houses out here, on a remote island on Christmas Eve? Farid had seen enough in life to make him cautious. He got to his feet, scanning the room in the darkness, his eyes settling on a roll of wrapping paper propped in the corner. Not the most effective weapon but better than nothing. He snatched it up, holding it in front of him like a lightsaber and tiptoeing out the door. Creeping across the corridor, he held his breath. *Please, no creaky floorboards.* The living room door was ajar. Farid stopped outside it, held his wrapping paper roll in front of him and peered around. His heart hammered. On the floor in front of the fireplace was a dark shape.

No way was that Santa Claus – not unless he'd lost weight and ditched the furry hat. Keeping his weapon in front, Farid tiptoed further into the room. His heartbeat was so loud the intruder might hear him. What should he do? Switch on the light? Go back to his room and call the police? Or grab him from behind? His feet had carried him to within a metre of the trespasser. He lowered the wrapping paper roll and poked the crouching figure in the shoulder. 'What are you doing?' he said, his voice low.

'Aarghhhh!' the person screamed, stumbling and groping on the floor. A blow hit the tube, almost knocking it from him.

He staggered back and flipped on the light.

Crouched on the rug was Holly, wielding a wrapped tube. 'God almighty.' She rubbed her chest. 'You gave me a heart attack.'

Farid raised an eyebrow. 'I gave you one? I'm not the one creeping around a house in the dark. What are you doing?'

She turned back to the rug, put the tube down, and stood up. Behind her, Farid spied a pile of presents on the floor in front of the grate. She held up her hands in surrender. 'I wanted to deliver your presents on Christmas Eve. I sneaked in and saw you were sleeping.'

Farid rubbed his forehead. 'I don't get it. Why are you giving me presents? Why are you even here?'

Holly pushed out her lips and glanced away. 'I made a mistake. I seem to do that quite a lot, but this time, I want to put it right before I lose everything I've always wanted.'

'Which is?'

'You.' She looked back at him, her eyes glistening. 'It might be too late for this and if it is, I accept the consequences, and on my own head be it. But, Farid...' She took a deep breath. '*Ana bahebak.*'

'Oh, *jamilati.*' Farid closed the gap between them and drew her into his chest. 'I love you too. Of course, it's not too late. I won't stop loving you that quickly. I won't stop loving you at all.'

She wrapped her arms around him and clung to him. 'I'm so undeserving of you. I messed up.'

'You just needed time.' He rested his cheek on hers. The warmth melted the lonely fingers gripping his heart, freeing his shoulders. He sighed into the crook of her neck. 'I can't ever say how much it means to me that you came back. Everything that has happened to me was part of a journey. The journey to you.'

'And I'm staying with you. I know now I can't be without you for long.'

'This is wonderful, *jamilati.* And I too have good news.' He rubbed his hand over her back. 'Archie has given me a computer. I will try to get my qualification to work in programming here. Then I can get a better job and we can go anywhere.'

'We're not going anywhere. We're staying here. This will be our home. For at least one year, I'm going to live here. We can go on trips and holidays, but our main home will be here.'

'Really?'

'It's my challenge. Every day we can remind each other of something we love about home.'

Farid kissed her cheek. 'And I will say the same thing every time. My home is wherever you are. You are my new home. My soul belongs with you. Together, we make one whole soul.'

'You are ridiculously romantic.'

'It's Christmas Eve. That's when the magic happens. It's true and it's not too late. We can still make a fire and cuddle. I even have nice chocolate and a fancy port, thanks to Per Hansen and his family.'

Holly stepped back and smiled. 'Oh god.' She gazed into his eyes. 'How could I ever have doubted how much I love you?'

He dipped his head and kissed her full on the lips. Worry or concern didn't temper the soaring joy tearing through his body. She was staying. They were free to make their home here, together. 'Let's not get carried away.'

'Why not? It always leads somewhere rather nice.' She trailed her finger down his cheek and across his short beard. He closed his eyes as she tripped her nail off the end of his chin.

'Yes, *jamilati*, but I want to sample the chocolate first and the port. I'm a little late to leave a carrot and a mince pie for the man in the red suit. He's been already.'

'You can't open them until tomorrow morning.'

'Ah, ok.'

'And it wasn't Santa anyway.'

'No?' He flipped her a sarcastic glance. 'I hope you're not trying to pretend it was you.'

'Of course not. We all know it isn't Santa who brings presents but an immortal camel.'

'Ahh, and was it him?'

Holly stepped aside and pointed to the rug. Farid looked properly for the first time at the pile of gifts. They were placed neatly around one of his work boots and a few of them were poking out of it. In front was a tiny carved wooden camel, lying down.

Farid stooped and picked it up. It was light as a feather and rich brown. 'This is gorgeous.'

'It's carved from an avocado stone. I saw it in a gift shop. I think it was made for you.'

'It's perfect. Like you, *jamilati.*' He held the camel in the palm of his hand. Placing it on his mantelpiece, he smiled. 'I'll treasure it.'

Holly slipped her fingers into his. 'Let's crack open this bottle then and we can toast our first Christmas together.'

The cupboards were stocked with every size and shape of glassware, including miniature wine glasses perfect for the port. Farid poured the ruby-red liquid and handed a glass to Holly. '*Eid milad sa'id,*' he said with a smirk.

Holly's lips quirked into a grin. 'I love you too.' She lifted her glass and sipped from it. 'And Merry Christmas.'

Chapter Thirty

Holly

Holly wasn't in the mood for getting up early on Christmas morning. Maybe one day, they'd be called at four in the morning by baby Farids and mini Hollys, but not yet. This was a morning to keep warm and how better to do it than with body heat? Farid's skin scorched with hot blood and Holly writhed beneath him in exquisite delight. His kisses and love penetrated deep inside her, lighting fires and warming her core.

She held him on top of her, breathing in his ear, their pulses racing in tandem. She couldn't stop smiling. He groaned and nuzzled her neck. Despite the darkness of the room, she knew he was grinning too.

When they finally got up, Holly nipped back to her cottage to shower and get dressed. In the kitchen, their Christmas cake sat on the worktop. She stared at it: the log symbolising Farid, her holly berries and leaves, and the love heart joining the two of them. An idea sprang into her head, paralysing her for a second. The memory of Gavin and the ring jarred her mind, and she frowned.

Her phone beeped and a message from Georgia popped up.

GEORGIA: Merry Christmas! I just had a message from Farid saying the two of you are back together and everything's going better than ever! I'm so happy and excited for you both. Don't be strangers. If you're fine on your own, that's great but if you want company, you're always welcome. XX

Georgia was so kind. Holly keyed out a message, saying everything was fine and they'd call round later, then picked up the cake and returned to Farid's side of the cottage.

Spicy aromas filled the room and Holly laid the cake on the breakfast bar, the mirror image of the one in her cottage. 'What are you making?'

'I will make my version of a Christmas lunch. I have some of your British favourites.' He held up a turkey crown and a stalk of sprouts.

'Sprouts?' Holly pulled a face.

'I will cook these in a way you will love. I promise, *jamilati,* you'll see.'

'And are you going to open your Christmas presents?'

'Of course, let me set this to cook, then I will open them. I'm sorry I have nothing for you. I would shower you with gold if I had it, *jamilati,* and give you everything I own. But what you see is what you get. I come with nothing.'

'That's ok. I quite like what I see... and even with nothing else, it's rather appealing.' She scanned him over from top to toe.

'Oh, Holly, you are still naughty.' He washed his hands and made his way around to the living room area.

'I have to warn you, it's traditional to get lots of nonsense in your Christmas stocking, so…' She threw up her hands. 'Sorry.'

'I'm sure I will love whatever it is.' He picked up the first gift and shook it. 'What do we have here?'

'You're not a feeler, are you?'

He raised an eyebrow and chuckled. 'I don't know. Am I?'

'It's someone who tries to guess what's inside their presents by fondling them all over first.'

'I'll save that for you.'

Holly smirked. 'Good plan.'

Farid pulled off the wrapping paper and held up a pair of socks. 'Amazing. What every man needs.'

'Exactly.' Holly watched as he opened the gifts, grinned at each one and ate half a packet of Matchmakers before moving to the next one.

'These are tasty,' he mumbled through a mouthful. 'But they might put me off my lunch.'

'That's another tradition. Stuff yourself with so much chocolate you can't eat your Christmas lunch, force it down anyway, come back for seconds, and spend the night dying on the sofa beside a bottle of Gaviscon. That's my father's way anyway.'

'Your traditions get stranger and stranger.'

'Don't they just.'

Farid picked up the final gift. 'The weapon. You almost knocked me out with this last night. What is it? A sword?'

'Eh, no.'

He ripped off the paper and pulled out the map tube. 'Oh, this is good. I like this. A map of our new home.'

Holly nodded, unable to say anything as a well of tears rose in her throat. Their home. She had a home with someone and it wasn't scary. The buzz crackling through her came from something different. The usual worries about where she was going next weren't there because she wasn't going anywhere. When work was done, she could switch off her laptop and go for a walk with Farid. 'We could get a puppy.'

Farid squinted up and frowned. 'What?'

'I always wanted a dog but my lifestyle didn't suit.'

Farid got off the rug and hopped onto the sofa next to Holly. His arms were around her and she was back in the happiest place in the world. 'Of course. I would love that. Our first baby.'

'Exactly.' She snuggled in and rested her head on him. 'Are we mad? I only met you a few weeks ago.'

'Life is short. Some people don't get the chances we have. I have lost many friends. This is a gift to both of us. We must accept it and use it. Let's not waste this chance, worrying what could go wrong. Let's take it and embrace what could go right.'

'The man who has a way with words.'

They held each other on the sofa while Holly processed what he'd said. It made sense. She'd given up on fate but something had brought her to Monarch's Lodge at the right moment for Farid to throw that elf costume at her. The second she'd seen him in his lumberjack shirt, her heart had raced off down the path of no return. She was well and truly on that road and it was exactly where she wanted to be.

'I'll always have space in my life for more programmers,' Holly said. 'You and I could work together. The project I'm doing for Robyn needs someone else alongside me.'

'You'd let me?'

'Why wouldn't I?'

'My qualification doesn't count here.'

'Screw that. Maybe it doesn't work for the corporate giants but for the self-employed among us, I'm happy to take you on merit. I saw your work the other day. The corporations would do well to let their applicants demonstrate their skills like that before picking the ones with the best on-paper qualifications.'

'Oh, *jamilati*, I'd love that. I miss the work.' His blue eyes twinkled.

'Then it's done.' She smiled.

He returned to the kitchen and Holly put on Classic FM, allowing herself to appreciate the gentle tones of Christmas carols. They didn't sound so painful anymore. More hopeful and comforting, like they'd plucked out the best parts of the past while also promising more in the future.

Holly set the breakfast bar ready for their Christmas feast with a difference.

'So, this is all my invention,' Farid said. 'We have the turkey kebabs instead of lamb. But let's go with it. And we have Fattoush, a delicious salad with tomatoes, peppers, celery and many more things. Now, here are the sprouts. I cook these using a recipe from the internet with pine nuts and maple syrup and I add some haloumi just for fun. We also have hummus, flatbread and olives.'

'This is possibly the strangest Christmas lunch I've ever had but it appeals to me more than usual. I'm always the weird one who doesn't like potatoes.'

'One day, I learn to cook them. I should try.'

'This will do for now.' Holly tucked in, enjoying the rainbow of flavours and grinning at the idea they'd created their own Christmas tradition. This was their own Christmas lunch. No one could take it from them. If they wanted hummus instead of Hellman's, so be it. The world wouldn't end tomorrow and they were still enjoying it. The carols played in the background until Holly and Farid were almost too full to move. With a great effort, they cleared up and flopped on the sofa, ready to watch any Christmas film that happened to be on. Mary Poppins would do.

Farid chuckled through it while Holly cringed. But enjoying time in his company was worth so much. After it finished, they got their coats and walked to the big house to exchange Merry Christmases with Georgia and Archie. Then they headed to the shore as the day waned. The sea lapped on the beach at the bottom of the steep path. Holly took Farid's bearded cheeks in her hands and pulled him in for a kiss. Waves chased the shore beyond and a lone bird let out a high cry. 'I'm so happy we're ok now,' she said.

'Me too. Let's get back before it's too dark to see.'

A flush of heat hit Holly's face as they returned to the house. 'Shall we have our cake now? Or can you not eat another thing?'

'I think we should.'

Holly slipped her hand into the back pocket of her jeans and felt a slip of paper under her fingertips. Her heartrate shot up. Did she have the nerve to do this? Was it tempting fate? It could fall flat on its face like the last time. The drumming of her heart increased as she peeled the film off the cake. 'Shall we cut it together?'

'Ok.' Farid wrapped his arms around her from behind, reminding her of how he'd done the same thing when they'd stirred the cake and she'd made a crazy wish. He placed both his hands over hers and together they slit the cake with a clean slice. It was like cutting a wedding cake. Farid kissed Holly's cheek. '*Bahebek, jamilati.*'

'I love you too. But I forgot plates.'

Farid left her and pulled out two plates. 'And I'll make a drink. Hot chocolate? Coffee? Tea?'

'Coffee.'

'Coming right up.'

Holly placed the slices of cake on the plate and then, checking Farid wasn't looking, slipped the piece of paper from her back pocket and pushed it under his piece of cake. She lifted both plates and held onto them until he had the coffee almost ready.

'Take a seat, *jamilati*. I'll bring this over.'

She moved to the sofa and put his plate on the coffee table. Her own plate sat firmly on her knee. She didn't want any chance of them getting mixed up. Farid brought over two cups neatly placed on saucers and laid them on the table.

'Let's see how good our cake made from tea is.' He leaned forward and picked up his plate. Holly felt sick. What if this was a terrible mistake? She laid her plate down. Even the sight of the cake made her want to throw up now. With trembling hands, she lifted the coffee instead. It wobbled on the saucer. Her lungs cinched; no air could get in. Farid's fingers were on the cake.

He lifted it towards his mouth and took a bite. 'Not bad.' He suspended the cake in mid-air, the folded slip of paper now clear on the plate. Spotting it, he frowned and swallowed the cake. 'What's this?' Returning the cake to the table, he touched the piece of paper.

Holly took a sip of coffee, her fingers trembling. Before she could replace the cup on the saucer, she saw something on it. Another piece of paper. 'What the...?' She glanced at Farid and he stared back. His expression levelled and he gave a tiny shrug.

'Maybe we should read them.'

Holly replaced her cup on the table and lifted the piece of paper. She unfolded it at the same time Farid unfurled his.

Will you be mine, forever, jamilati?

'Oh, my god.' Holly clutched her face in both her hands, desperately pushing back tears. Of all the surprises, she could never have predicted this. Farid was staring at his own note, half-frowning, half-smiling. Then he turned to her and grinned.

'I'll say yes to you if you say yes to me.'

Tears rolled down Holly's cheek as she threw her arms around him. 'Yes.'

'*Ay, na'am.* I will be yours forever. With all my heart. It's the greatest honour.'

'I guess you understood my note. I'm not sure Google translate is the most accurate.'

'I understood perfectly. I just hope you can accept me for the man of no means that I am.'

'Easily. Because you accept me for the grumpy, stubborn woman that I am.'

He slipped a strand of hair behind her ear. 'I wouldn't have you any other way. It's what makes you you. And I want nothing but you.'

'Likewise. Woman can't survive on love alone but it bloody well helps to make her feel good.'

Farid smirked and swayed her gently from side to side. 'I understand Christmas better now.'

'And do you like it?'

'I like it with you. It's not about turkeys, puddings, lights and bells. It's about being with people you love.'

'And I can say the same about home. Home doesn't mean being tied to a place. It's about the warmth, comfort and support of other people.'

'Together we're stronger, *jamilati*. We can take on the world, make a home and have many more Christmases and celebrations of our own. As long as we're together, we can do anything.'

'Amen to that.' She tilted her head and smiled at him, enjoying the glint of stars in his bright blue eyes before he closed them, dipped in and sealed his lips with hers.

The End

MORE BOOKS BY MARGARET AMATT

Scottish Island Escapes

1. A Winter Haven

2. A Spring Retreat

3. A Summer Sanctuary

4. An Autumn Hideaway

5. A Christmas Bluff

6. A Flight of Fancy

7. A Hidden Gem

8. A Striking Result

9. A Perfect Discovery

10. A Festive Surprise

The Glenbriar Series

1. Stolen Kisses at the Loch View Hotel

2. Just Friends at Thistle Lodge

3. Pitching up at Heather Glen

4. Two's Company at the Forest Light Show

5. Highland Fling on the Whisky Trail

6. Snowdown at the Old Schoolhouse

7. Starting Over at the Crafty Bee Barn

8. A Surprise Proposal in the Rose Garden

9. Cutting it Neat for the Wedding

10. A Classy Affair in the Country

11. Mix Up under the Mistletoe

12. A Fresh Start on the Bridle Path

ABOUT THE AUTHOR
Margaret Amatt

Margaret has told and written stories for as long as she can remember. During her formative years, she spent time on long walks inventing characters and stories to pass the time.

Writing books is Margaret's passion and when she's not doing that, she's often found eating chocolate, walking and taking photographs in the hills around Highland Perthshire. Those long walks still frequently bring inspiration!

It's Margaret's pleasure to bring you the Scottish Island Escapes series and The Glenbriar Series. These books are linked (both the two series have crossovers!) for those who enjoy inhabiting Margaret's world of stories but each book can be read as a standalone if you'd rather dip in and out.

You can find more information about Margaret on her website or by signing up for her newsletter.

www.margaretamatt.com

Acknowledgments

Thanks goes to my adorable husband for supporting my dreams and putting up with my writing talk 24/7. Also to my son, whose interest in my writing always makes me smile. It's precious to know I've passed the bug to him – he's currently writing his own fantasy novel and instruction books on how to build Lego!

Throughout the writing process, I have gleaned help from many sources and met some fabulous people. I'd like to give a special mention to Stéphanie Ronckier, my beta reader extraordinaire. Stéphanie's continued support with my writing is invaluable and I love the fact that I need someone French to correct my grammar! Stéphanie, you rock. To my lovely friend, Lyn Williamson, thank you for your continued support and encouragement with all my projects. And to my fellow authors, Evie Alexander and Lyndsey Gallagher – you girls are the best! I love it that you always have my back and are there to help when I need you.

Also, a thanks to the editors at Leannan Press for their work on this novel.

Of course a huge thank you goes to the readers who continue to support me in so many ways. I appreciate each and every one of you and hope that I can keep bringing you more books to enjoy! Big love.

Margaret XX

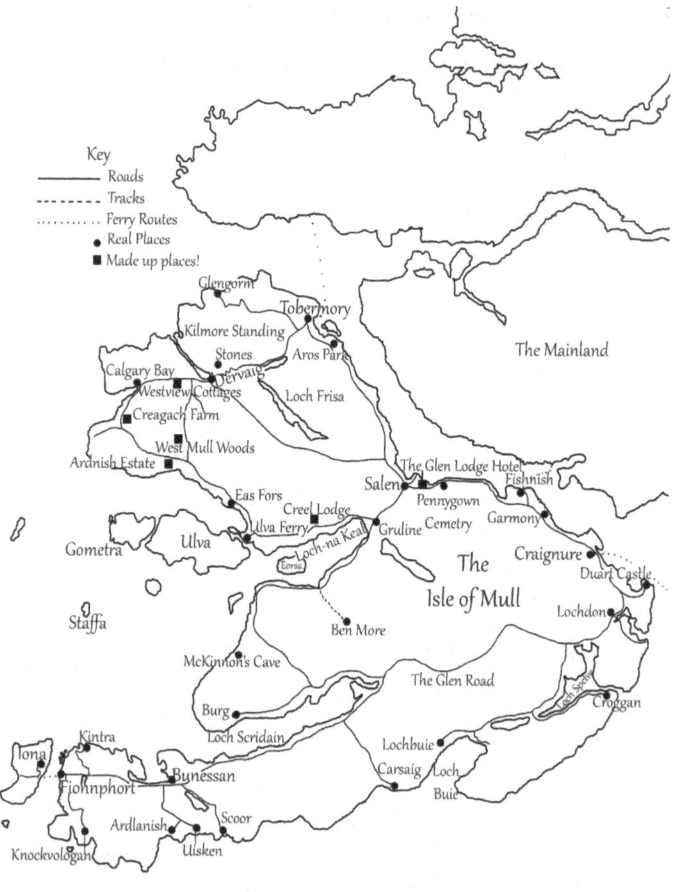

The Isle of Mull where the Scottish Island Escapes series is set